KEY LIME CRIME

SUNNY SHORES MYSTERIES BOOK 1

CASSIE RIVERS

D1502000

The following short story is a work of fiction. Any similarities to real people, events, or places are entirely coincidental. Happy Reading!

I welcome you to sign up for my mailing list to be informed of new releases and special discounts. I also giveaway a free mystery to anyone who joins. I hate spam myself, so you don't have to worry about me clogging your inbox. I rarely send out more than two emails a month. Click the link below to join.

CLICK HERE

CONTENTS

My grandmother often told me that when life gives you lemons, make lemonade. Solid advice, but I'm more of a lime girl myself.

Unfortunately for me over the last year, all I received was sour grapes.

I had returned to my hometown, Sunny Shores, Florida, after being away for six years. Although I'd been gone, most things seemed unchanged from when I left. While the tourism boom brought in many new faces, our small, cozy beach town was as full of unique characters and personalities as before. Each person had their own unique story to tell as well as their own secrets or demons to hide.

My father often said everyone, no matter who they were, was hiding something. He believed the only distinction was to what degree and seriousness their secrets truly were. Having been a detective most of his life, he would've known that better than anyone.

Memorial Day marked the beginning of another busy summer tourist season, which the many local businesses and merchants were looking forward to. For most, the income earned from the summer months carried them through the rest of the year.

The summer marked a new beginning. The possibilities seemed endless. That summer marked the beginning of a new chapter in my life as well. After a series of unfortunate and untimely events, I had moved back to my hometown.

This was not the way I'd pictured my life being at this point.

I had a clear path mapped out for my life, and I'd planned it out to a tee. It was the perfect plan, or at least I thought it was.

I'd finish law school, marry my high school sweetheart, open our own law firm, and pop out a few kids. You know... the whole white picket fence ordeal.

Those dreams shattered with the sudden passing of my father the year before.

Some say death breeds new life. For me that was true. His death gave me something that I hadn't previously had. The gift was the true perspective on what's important in life. That was family. So I dropped out of law school and put any relationship needs of my own on hold.

At twenty-three years old, I found myself single and unemployed. Like a ship stranded in the middle of the ocean, I drifted, clueless. I lacked direction about what to do or where to go next.

My only choice was to chart a new course in life. It was time to make the best out of a bad situation. So I took my mother's lemonade advice.

It didn't have to be law school or bust for me, because I wasn't without other talents. A couple tricks remained up my sleeves. My vocabulary lacked the word quit.

The truth was that there was something very special about me. It was something that made me stand out from all the other people in the town. It was a secret so deadly I would have to take it to the grave.

You see, I'm a witch…

Just kidding. I'd like to think my food tasted spell-binding. Although I do have this magic trick where guys I like tend to disappear, but I digress.

I loved to cook, so I decided to go with a backup plan. Ever since I was a little girl, I'd dreamed of opening my own bakery. Since I couldn't afford a bakery, I went with the next best idea. That was to open my own food truck. It was a risky venture, but at this point, I needed to take a few risks.

With the help of my newly hired employee, Star, and childhood best friend, Ty, my goal was to open for business on Memorial Day. My truck needed only a few final touches, including introducing them to the truck.

"Lady and gentleman, may I present... the new Burger She Wrote food truck."

In my mind, I'd imagined great joy and applause. Instead, my announcement met with a reaction of uncertainty and disdain. Neither one seemed to share in my enthusiasm.

"That ugly piece of junk," Star replied with a look of utter disgust painted on her face. "You're joking, right?"

"It's definitely a fixer-upper," Ty said, trying to stay positive as usual. "But it's a good start."

"I'll admit that it's not perfect, but all it needs is a little TLC."

"What it needs… is to be pushed into the ocean, to put it out of its misery," said Star.

Ty turned to Star and said, "It's not that bad. Don't be so dramatic."

"Remind me what you're doing here again? Aren't you an accountant? Shouldn't you be crunching numbers, counting beans, or whatever you nerds do?"

Ty and I had been best friends since the third grade. He'd recently passed the state CPA exam. Earlier in the year, he took a job as an associate at Henderson's Accounting Firm. The busy tax season was over, so he had a lot of free time. Although I insisted he didn't have to, Ty volunteered to help me out as much as he could.

I'll admit that the truck didn't look like much, but it was exactly what I needed at the time. Owning my own bakery was my main goal at this point, but there was no way I could afford that. You might have figured that on your own. My current situation of being a twenty-three year old unemployed law school drop-out living at home with my mother didn't help.

Fortunately for me, I'd scored a good deal on an older, used food truck.

"Older things are in style now, right? What's the word everyone uses?" I asked.

"Retro?" Ty answered.

"Yes, that's the word," I said.

Star shook her head. "That's not the word I'd use to describe it."

I purchased 1980 Chevrolet step van from an advertisement on Craigslist. The vehicle was originally used for bread deliveries.The previous owner converted the van into a food truck. In my eyes, the truck had potential. It had little body damage, only a few small dings and scratches.

In an effort to save money, the previous owner had raided junkyards to find replacement parts for the vehicle, so the van was multicolored. None of the wheels matched. It had so many mismatched parts it looked like something created by Dr. Frankenstein in a lab—while drunk.

Star shook her head as she stood in disbelief. It was crystal clear by the annoyed look on her face that she was not impressed.

I had only known Star Daniels for a few days, but it felt like I'd known her my entire life. Star was eighteen and fresh out of high school. She needed a summer job to save money before going to college in the fall.

She had only lived in Sunny Shores for a year, but due to her personality and style, she was well known throughout the town. You honestly couldn't miss her. Star stood tall and stunningly beautiful with bright pink hair. She was the type of person that drew attention whenever she entered a room, whether the attention was good or bad.

Star was the type of person that didn't hold back. She was blunt and to the point. She wasn't afraid to let you know how she felt.

And beneath all that, she was truly genuine. I felt every word she said she meant. In that sense, she seemed very trustworthy.

Besides, she complemented my personality in the perfect way. I considered her bluntness and brashness a good thing, even though some of the more traditional people in town took her as being rude over everything else. I knew better. Her heart was usually in the right place.

"When I answered your help wanted ad, you stated that you needed someone to help with your small restaurant business. Your ad failed to mention I'd be working out of a creepy looking death-box."

Ty smiled. "Star, didn't your mother ever teach you not to judge a book by its cover? It's what's on the inside that counts."

"Let's not get started on my mother, that's what my therapist is for," Star replied.

I opened the back door to the Burger She Wrote food truck and said, "Take a look inside."

The inside of the truck remained clean and well maintained for an older vehicle. The previous owner had recently renovated the inside and added all new appliances. But due to unfortunate circumstances, they'd failed to finish remodeling the exterior of the truck. The owner left the truck an unfinished mess.

On the bright side, the truck was fully equipped for most of my needs. On the left side, a large window functioned to serve the food to guests. The grill sat directly behind the window, on the right side wall. In the front was a prep area that included a stainless steel countertop and two sinks. A small refrigerator and a freezer were tucked up under the counters.

The truck housed one broken item that bothered me the most. One of the two ovens failed to heat up. I lacked the necessary funds to fix it. Since baking was my passion, this was a bit disheartening. I had to arrive early each morning to ensure enough time to bake my desserts.

"Hmm," Star muttered under her breath as she stepped inside. She looked around and inspected it before replying. "This could work, but you have to do something about the outside of this thing. You can't expect me to be seen in something as hideous as this."

"You don't have to worry about that, Star," I said. "I have a plan."

"My sister's boyfriend works at Tom's Body Shop. She can score us a great deal," Ty interjected.

"Or…" I said as I pulled out two cans of spray paint from under the counter. "We could save money and do it ourselves."

Spray painting the truck wasn't the best idea, but it was all I could afford. It didn't matter, anyway. I had ordered enough cute decals to stick all over the outside of my truck. These included a large cartoon hamburger, a magnifying glass, and the letters to spell out the name. I didn't doubt for a minute that the finished product would look great.

"Lime green?" Star said as she examined the spray paint can in her hand. "Really? Of all the colors you could've chosen."

Ty laughed. "Your favorite color. I should have known."

"Let's get going. I'll run to the store to get the last of the supplies, and you two can finish painting. Hopefully, it'll be dry by morning, and we can stick the decals on before we open," I said as my phone began to ring.

Pulling my cell phone out of my pocket, I took a quick glance at the screen. Nonchalantly, I read the caller ID to see who was calling. I already had a hunch about who it was without looking.

"It's him again, isn't it?" Ty asked while shaking his head. "Dusty."

"It was Dustin," I said as I fiddled nervously with my phone and put it in my purse. His name was Dustin, not Dusty. I hated when people referred to him by that name.

"Who's Dustin?" Star asked.

"No time for small talk now. We have a lot to do," I said as I gathered my keys and walked out of the truck. I desperately tried to change the subject since I already knew Ty's opinion on Dustin. Even though my head knew he was right, my heart thought differently.

Ty walked over to Star and spoke quietly in her ear. "I'll explain later. I have a feeling we'll have plenty of time to talk while trying to paint this entire truck tonight."

Like I said before, my little cozy beach town was full of people with secrets and demons. I never said it didn't include me as well.

2

I f there was one common complaint my friends and family had with me, it was that I was too boring and predictable. I was notorious for being an over-planner. Most called my outlook on life boring, but I preferred the word stable. Was it so awful I wanted to stick to a consistent routine?

As part of my boring... normal routine each morning, I walked to work. It wasn't a long walk since my mother's house sat only two miles from Grove Park. The walk provided great exercise and helped keep me in decent shape. It was difficult enough trying to keep the pounds off while spending the majority of the day cooking. To make matters worse, the beach was full of life-size Barbie dolls parading around in skimpy bikinis.

The morning walk provided a meditating effect as well. I found my morning stroll calm and relaxing, as it was a great way to clear my head. The walk allowed me to mentally prepare for the long day ahead. Experiencing the cool morning breeze from the ocean and scent from the orange groves was a great way to start the morning.

The operating hours for my food truck were from 11 a.m. until 8 p.m. On a normal workday, I would leave my home at 6 a.m. and not return home until after 9 p.m. It was a long day.

Without caffeine, I wouldn't be able to function on the busy summer schedule. So each morning, my first stop was the Breezy Bean Café.

The Breezy Bean Café was a local coffee shop located downtown, on the corner of Ocean Avenue and Orange Way. The shop itself was small and only had room for a long rectangular counter and five four-top tables.

But in the case of the Breezy Bean Café, size really didn't matter. The Breezy Bean was one of the more popular downtown establishments in Sunny Shores. The shop was very busy during peak hours due to its close location to the beach and magnificent coffee.

Bonnie May Calloway owned and operated the Breezy Bean Café. She'd lived in Sunny Shores her entire life. Besides owning a local business, Bonnie May held a position as one of the town council members.

Bonnie May never admitted to anyone her true age.I would guess she was in her fifties, but she had the demeanor and energy of someone in her twenties. She had never married or had any children of her own. This may have been the secret to her youth-fulness.

"That's a lovely new perm, Bonnie May," I told her as I sipped my morning coffee. "What color is that?"

"It's called buttered toast, or at least that's what my hairdresser told me."

Bonnie May went to the hairdresser more times in one year than I had in my entire lifetime. Every time you turned around, her hair would be a different color or style.

I smiled and asked, "Do you even remember what the original color of your hair was?"

"Auburn... I think," she said. We both began to laugh.

"Excuse me," called a voice from a table behind me. "I'm in a big hurry. Could you bring me my check? Preferably sometime this century."

Bonnie May put her head down and mumbled under her breath, "I'll give you something, you little..."

The voice from the back corner of the café was that of Missy Harmon. Missy was the wife of city councilman John Harmon. She was staring straight at Bonnie May, obnoxiously waving her American Express black card around in the air.

I didn't know Missy or her husband well. They'd both moved to Sunny Shores during the time I was away at school. What little I knew about Missy was that she was at best a trophy wife. She didn't seem to do anything else but go around town spending her husband's money.

"Coming right up, dear," Bonnie May replied after taking a deep breath. She managed to conjure a smile on her face and appeared unfazed by the level of rudeness displayed by Missy.

She took Missy's card back over to the register to process it, and turned to me and whispered, "Never let them see you sweat, Kara. As long as the checks clear or the credit card's approved, the joke is on them."

"Have a blessed day," Bonnie said as she handed Missy her card and a credit card slip to sign.

Missy walked to the counter and slammed her credit card receipt in front of Bonnie May. The entire time, she had her cell phone to her ear, avoiding any eye contact with Bonnie May. As she left the restaurant, she made sure to raise her voice so Bonnie May could catch the last part of her conversation.

"Why can't we get a Starbucks around here?"

"That woman is unreal," Bonnie May said as she picked up the signed credit card receipt. "Just look at what she wrote."

Missy not only signed the credit card slip but left a note as well.

"Coffee was OK, but service was slow."

According to Bonnie May, Missy did this every time.

"I don't know what's more annoying, the note or her prissy signature," I said as I examined the receipt.

"What's her deal?"

"My guess would be that she's new money."

"New money?"

"It's when someone originally has little or no money, then later inherits a fortune or marries into it. Because they've lived most of their lives without money, they have to flaunt it in front of everyone."

"I'm surprised her husband is so well off. Does his restaurant do that great?"

"His restaurant business has been down in the last couple of years. In fact, your little group of food truck friends almost put him out of business. Why do you think he started a truck of his own?"

"From what I heard, he made his fortune in real estate. The restaurant business is just a side venture for him."

"Maybe so, but he's a very competitive person. Most would say to a fault. He's the type that won't rest until he's number one."

I laughed. "I don't think I have much to worry about then. I'm not getting rich anytime soon, based on my sales so far."

I finished up my coffee and settled up with Bonnie May. I could sit and talk all day, but a lot of work needed to be done before I opened the truck. So I walked over to Grove Park to begin my day.

~

Today was like any other day since I began my foray into the food truck business. It was 8:15 a.m. and Grove Park was quiet. As I began to whip cream with my spatula, the only sound I could hear was the swaying of the orange groves from the cool ocean breeze.

The Burger She Wrote food truck had been opened for business about two weeks, and business boomed.

I named it the Burger She Wrote food truck for a couple of reasons. It was a play on words based on the Murder She Wrote television series. I must have seen every episode a hundred times each. My typical Friday night was a Netflix and chill night. I binge watched Murder She Wrote on Netflix while chilling with a few glasses of chardonnay. I stopped telling this to people once Star explained to me that Netflix and chill had another, more scandalous meaning.

The other obvious reason was that it was a food truck that served hamburgers. I'll admit that selling hamburgers and fries from a food truck wasn't my first choice, but no other truck in the park offered this option. Burgers and fries seemed like a natural fit for a tourist destination visited by families with kids.

Although I cooked a pretty darn good hamburger if I say so myself, the main draw of my business was the desserts. Creating cupcakes, pies, cakes, and other tasty treats had been a passion of mine since I was a child using my Easy Bake Oven.

I tried to incorporate this into my business by offering a standard dessert menu, as well as a special dessert of the day. It wasn't unusual for me to sell out of my dessert items shortly after lunch.

Although I didn't officially open for business until 11 a.m., there was a ton of work that had to be done in preparation. Because I insisted on having baked goods prepared daily, my day started around 8 a.m. There had to be plenty of time to do the mixing, baking, and decorating involved in crafting the perfect treat. Most of my deserts required baking, which took longer than cooking something on the grill. Having only one oven slowed things down as well.

For these reasons, I was normally the first food truck owner at the park each morning. That was why it was a surprise to hear a loud voice shouting in the distance. I put down my spatula and peeked out the large window of the truck. It was Carlos Martinez talking to his wife.

My nosy tendencies wouldn't allow me to keep my nose in my business. That would have been too easy. Carlos Martinez and his wife Maria operated the Loco Taco truck, which sat parked in the lot next to mine.

"You two are here early this morning," I said as I walked in front of their truck. "Is everything OK?"

"It's nothing, Kara," Maria replied as Carlos continued to mutter words under his breath in Spanish."My hot-head of a husband is stressing over nothing."

"Nothing?!" Carlos exclaimed, a vein looking like it was about to pop out of his head. I'm not sure if I'd ever seen anyone's face turn that shade of red before. "Our sales are down over thirty percent since that crook stole my spot. That is not nothing."

"Do you think our sales are really going to matter if you have a heart attack or a stroke?" Maria said as she put her arms around him. "The doctor told you that added stress wasn't good for your heart. He said you needed to calm down. Remember the breathing exercise?"

Carlos took a deep breath. "I know. It's just frustrating. I spent years building my business only to have someone cheat their way ahead of me."

In all honesty, Carlos spoke the truth.

Grove Park was the access point to the Sunny Shores public beach, which was the main tourist draw of the town. Besides the beach itself, the town's new boardwalk recently opened adjacent to the park. The park provided plenty of parking for guests and stayed full the majority of the summer.

In a stroke of genius three years back, Carlos figured out what Grove Park was missing. Food.

The closest restaurants or dining establishments were located downtown. Although it wasn't a long walk from the park, it was inconvenient for many families with small children.

No one had tried to build a restaurant closer to the park due to the lack of open space and available land. There just wasn't enough room to open a full-size restaurant. Carlos saw this and dreamed up the idea to open a food truck business inside the park.

The idea for starting a food truck business came into Carlos's head while watching a reality show on the Food Network. The show was a competition between various food truck owners. On that episode, the competitors parked near a beach. This set off a light in Carlos's head.

Carlos wasted no time and purchased a food truck of his very own. With the approval of the city council, he acquired a permit to park in a grassy lot, adjacent to the public beach entrance. He dubbed his truck the Loco Taco and sold delicious tacos and other Mexican specialties.

As it turned out, his food truck was a hit. It was so busy that he couldn't keep up with demand. This caused other people in the town to take notice.Soon others opened food trucks of their own. By the second summer of operation, there were five independent food trucks set up in Grove Park.

Since everyone respected Carlos for starting the trend, no one tried to take his spot. It was an unwritten code between food truck owners. Once someone claimed a spot, each owner respected the other's boundaries. That was until the lottery.

One councilman, John Harmon, introduced a bill to assign lots to specific food trucks by doing a random lottery. The town council conveniently held the lottery drawing behind closed doors. Even more convenient than that, the Mama Mia Italian food truck received the most coveted lot space, Carlos's spot. Coincidentally enough, the Mama Mia Italian truck was owned by John Harmon himself.

Obviously, Carlos had every right to be upset with the town council, especially with John Harmon.

"Hang in there, Carlos," I said, trying to defuse the situation. "You make the best tacos this side of the Atlantic. Things will turn around soon. I'm sure of it."

We exchanged a few more pleasantries, and then I headed back to my truck to finish the last of the prep work. At the same time, Star showed up for work. We would spend the next few hours getting ready for the lunch rush.

"What are you doing here on a Tuesday?" I asked as Len Arlen walked up to the window of my truck. "I thought you only delivered here on Thursdays."

Len Arlen was in my grade growing up. His father owned the local propane dealership, and he went to work with him after graduation. Len's company delivered once a week to the park on Thursday. Seeing him so early in the week was unusual.

"That's normally the case, but the Loco Taco and another truck ordered an additional delivery. For some reason, they needed an extra tank. I'm not going to argue because it's more money for us."

"That's true."

"Besides, it gives me an excuse to drop by for a piece of your Key lime pie."

One of the perks of owning my own food truck was the opportunity to meet and interact with a variety of people, including friends I grew up with. In addition, I enjoyed chatting with the tourists that came through Grove Park each day. My business afforded me the opportunity to meet people from all walks of life.

My truck was not only visited by tourists, but by the town folks as well. The people of Sunny Shores were an interesting bunch, to say the least. I was enjoying getting reacquainted with the people of the town, but there were a few I wasn't so happy to see.

3

"**W**ell if it isn't little Kara-bear," said a familiar voice, while my back faced the window. "I'd heard through the grapevine you were back in town."

Oh, great, I thought, as I paused a moment before responding.

I knew who it was without taking a peek. It was none other than the Mayor of Sunny Shores himself, Mr. Roy Coltrane, otherwise known as my ex-boyfriend's father. I'd not seen or spoken with Mr. Coltrane since the breakup.

As a way to help shake the awkwardness off, I took a deep breath, then put on a fake smile before turning around.

It didn't help.

"Hi, Mr. Coltrane," I said. "How are you this morning?"

Mr. Coltrane, while loud and brash, was a short, portly man. If you'd ever watched the show The Dukes of Hazzard, he looked and acted like Boss Hog himself. He strutted around the town in his trademark white cowboy hat and bright Hawaiian shirts.

"How many times have I told you, Kara? Call me Roy. Mr. Coltrane sounds so formal. Besides, you were always like a daughter to me," he replied. "Actually, you almost were until you two broke up."

"About that, Roy. I'm sorry I've never had a chance to explain. I had a lot going on at the time, and I…"

Before I could finish explaining, Mayor Roy interrupted as if he didn't care what I had to say. In fact, his son was exactly the same way. The apple didn't fall from the tree in that regard.

"No need to explain anything to me, darling. I know how women can be sometimes. I've married three, so I have experience," he said as he began to chuckle.

As he laughed, his belly jiggled like a bowl of jello.

"Excuse me?" Star said, as she couldn't take listening to him any longer. "What's your problem with Kara?"

"Oww wee, who's this little firecracker?" he said in a creepy, stranger-in-a-van type of way. "She's a feisty one."

Star responded by giving Mayor Roy the stare of death. Her emerald green eyes could have pierced a hole through him. I quickly spoke up before she could say anything else.

"This is Star. She's helping run the truck this summer."

Mayor Roy looked over in Star's direction and smiled. "When Kara gives up this silly dream and comes back to reality, I may be looking for an intern. Think about it, sweetheart."

He gave Star a wink. Taking a gander at Mayor Roy, you wouldn't take him for being the obnoxious flirt he was. The job of mayor and power that the office held went straight to his bald head. He acted as if he were untouchable. Unfortunately for him, Star was about to test that theory with a slap across his face.

I could see Star getting angrier by the second. The last thing I needed was my employee assaulting the town's mayor, even if he deserved it. To calm the tension, I changed the subject as swiftly as I could.

"So what can I get for you this morning, Roy?"

"Hmm… I'm a bit hungry, now that you mention it," he said as his eyes glanced over to the glass case where the blueberry muffins were sitting.

"I'll have one of those muffins and a large Coke."

"Star, will you fix the Mayor's drink, while I ring him up?"

Star whispered under her breath, "I'll fix him alright…"

"That'll be four dollars and fifty cents," I said as I handed him his muffin.

He opened his wallet and pulled out a five dollar bill. "Keep the change, girls," he said as he slammed the bill on the counter.

Star begrudgingly handed him his soda. He tipped his hat and went on his way.

"Why do you let him talk to you that way?" Star asked. "It's not like you're dating his son anymore. You don't need to take his crap."

"My grandmother always said you catch more flies with honey."

Star shook her head. "My grandmother said revenge is a dish best served cold."

He'd intimidated me from the moment I met him. My ex thought it was silly when I told him how I felt about his father, but it was serious to me. In his eyes, I never felt like I was good enough for his son.

"He's gone now, so it doesn't matter now. No use in worrying about it."

"If you say so," Star replied. "But if it makes you feel any better, I gave him Diet Coke instead of regular. Maybe he'll get the hint."

4

"Order up," Star yelled back as she placed the order ticket on the counter. "One Bacon and Clue Cheese medium well, hold the mayo. Side of cheese fries."

"Cheese fries?" I asked. "I don't recall that being on the menu. Are you sure you're getting the name right?"

"Seriously, Kara?" She sighed heavily before reluctantly replying. "Pardon me. One order of Cheese Fries and Alibis." She rolled her eyes, as I tried to keep a straight face.

I knew good and well what she was referring to, but I wanted her to say the correct name. A lot of time and effort went into creating those names.

Corny or not, the names played into the theme of the truck.

Truth be told, I needed to worry about the grill more than Star's lack of enthusiasm. Orders stacked up fast, as the line grew to five people deep. I felt trapped in the weeds.

Although I loved baking the best, I grew to enjoy the chaos of manning the grill. It tested my skills of multitasking each day, but I loved it. Staying busy made the time fly by. In addition to that, the busier we were, the more money I was earning. In other words, one step closer to owning my dream café downtown.

The Bacon and Clue Cheese burger was the daily special and proved to be a favorite among the tourists and locals. The burger consisted of a fresh half-pound Angus beef patty with melted crumbled blue cheese, direct from the local dairy farm. I finished it off with crispy, applewood bacon and a homemade citrus chipotle BBQ sauce.

I learned to appreciate the period of time between the end of lunch rush and beginning of dinner. Those few hours provided much needed downtime. Business in the park slowed to a crawl, with a few customers trickling in from time to time.

At that point in the day, most day tourists headed home. Grove Park became calm and quieter. On most days you could hear the waves breaking in the distance, with faint sounds of children laughing and playing in the surf.

Star cleaned around the truck, while I restocked and prepped for dinner. I enjoyed this time for other reasons as well. It allowed an opportunity for Star and me to talk and get to know each other better.

"So what really happened to you?" Star asked as she glanced up from the sink. "I'm still trying to comprehend your reasoning for dropping out of school mid-semester."

"It's complicated."

"Don't get me wrong, I'm totally being selfish here, but I'm glad you did. I desperately needed a job," she said. "I can't believe you walked away from a full scholarship to law school."

"Who told you that?"

"Ty."

"What else has he told you?" I asked.

"I just figured that we should try to open up to each

other, since we're going to be working so close all summer."

I answered her with the same stock answer I'd given everyone else who asked. "We were high school sweethearts who grew apart."

I kept the true reason hidden from everyone. Not even my mother or best friend knew the real truth as to why we broke up.

"Cut the crap, Kara,"

I racked my brain for a witty response. Nothing came.

"He changed, and I didn't," I explained. "In high school, he was funny, sweet, and charming. I fell head over heels for him."

"And then?"

"It wasn't an abrupt change, but it occurred in subtle doses. Before I knew it, he was cold and heartless. Our plans didn't matter. Everything was about him, and how he could get ahead. No matter who he had to hurt to get there. Including me."

"That does suck," Star replied. "Do you think people really change? Or do they eventually reveal their true selves?"

That was an excellent question which I didn't have an answer to.

I continued. "And when my father died, a moment in which I really needed him, he wasn't there for me."

"What about Ty?" she asked. "You two seem to get along well. I'm shocked that you two haven't dated. You both seem to be a match."

I laughed. "Me and Ty? You're funny."

"Why's that so funny? You both are dorky and cute together."

I wasn't sure if that was a compliment or an insult. Ty and I had been friends since I moved to Sunny Shores as a child. At this point, imagining him as anything other than a friend seemed weird.

"We were boyfriend and girlfriend in the third grade, but only for one day."

"What happened?"

"He stole my Ninja turtle doll."

Before I could continue, we heard a loud commotion from the other side of the park.

"Who the hell do you think you are?" screamed a voice from across the quad.

Curious, Star and I walked outside the truck. We crept a few yards closer to get a better peek. We were doing our parts as concerned citizens. Wait, who was I kidding? We were just being nosy neighbors.

"I do everything around here," the other voice shouted. "I deserve some respect. Give me some appreciation for crying out loud."

"I give you a lot of things, including a job. No one else would. You should be thanking me."

The fighting and screaming originated from behind the Mama Mia food truck. The two who caused the ruckus were John Harmon and his step-son Chris. Both men stood directly in front of one another, both shouting in each other's face.

"That's odd," Star whispered as we both hid behind a palmetto tree. "John Harmon hasn't shown his face around Grove Park since the grand opening of his truck."

With so many of the food truck owners furious with him over stealing their spots, avoiding Grove Park seemed a smart decision.

"You've been drinking again, haven't you?" Chris said as he pointed his finger in John's face. John responded by slapping Chris's hand away with his right hand. "I smell it on your breath."

"That's none of your concern," he replied in a snarky tone. "With having a worthless and pathetic step-son like you, who'd blame me?"

The more I listened to John talk, the more I noticed his speech was slurred. On top of that, his face appeared red and bloated. He also was overly animated with his gestures while talking. Maybe he was drunk.

Of the two, Chris tried to keep his cool. Although with each hate-laced insult, his gaze intensified. I started to wonder if someone should step in and ease the tension. The last thing we needed was a fist fight in Grove Park. Or worse, the impending video going viral on YouTube.

"You think we should do something?" I whispered to Star. "It's getting pretty heated over there."

"Are you kidding?" she replied. "This is just getting good."

"I don't think I'm being unreasonable, John," Chris said, patiently holding his ground. "Business is booming and we have the money."

John shook his head in disgust. He brushed Chris off and made a gesture with his hand.

"I don't have time for this," he said as he turned his back and stormed off. John had a slight stumble in his step as he made his way to his black BMW 7 series sedan.

John wasted no time in leaving. He started his car and revved the engine loud. His tires squealed, leaving only a trail of dust and a ticked off step-son behind. His car shot out of the parking lot and barely missed hitting a man on a bicycle.

"What got up into his craw?" Star asked as we watched his car disappear in the distance.

I drew a blank. The only thing certain was that John left Chris in a foul mood as well. He slammed the door as he stomped his way inside the truck.

I didn't know Chris that well at the time, since he moved to Sunny Shores around the time I was away at school. From our few interactions in the park, he seemed mild-mannered and balanced. That wasn't the case today. Chris was furious.

"Let's go over and talk to him," I suggested. I felt it was the neighborly thing to do. "He seems very upset."

"That's a big negative on that one," Star replied.

"Why not?" I asked.

"If you must know, we went on a date a few weeks back. It was before you came back to town."

"You dated Chris Kelly?" I asked.

"No" she shouted. By the tone in her voice, it seemed that I'd insulted her. "I went on a date with him, only one."

"So what's the big deal?"

"The big deal is I never called him back or responded to his texts."

"That's awful. If you weren't interested in him, why not let him know? Why keep the poor guy in suspense?"

"That's not how dating works now. You don't tell someone directly you're not interested. The trick is to fade away slowly. The term is ghosting."

"Ghosting?"I asked. "Great. Another new dating term."

"Ghosting is when you just vanish out of their lives. No calls, texts, emails. To them, it's like you disappeared into thin air. Like a ghost."

Her statement summed up, in a nutshell, why I avoided dating. With so many codes and rules, who could keep up? My head spun trying to comprehend it all.

"Fine. I'll go alone."

As I approached the Mama Mia food truck, I heard the sound of objects being slung around inside. Chris mumbled obscenities under his breath as he paced around.

"Knock, knock," I said as I stuck my head in the main window. "Is everything OK in there?"

Startled by my sudden appearance, he stopped pacing and turned toward me. Chris, embarrassed by what had previously transpired, turned red in the face. In the midst of the screaming and fighting, I figured he failed to realize they had an audience.

"You heard all that?" he asked as he bit his upper lip.

"Everyone in Sunny Shores heard that," I replied. "You two weren't exactly being discreet."

"He's just so frustrating," he said as he noticeably started to get worked up again. "Sometimes I want to ring his neck and choke his lights out."

He obviously harbored a deep disdain for his step-father. His comment seemed a bit extreme and violent. It didn't help matters that he pretended to choke the air in front of him with his hands.

I started to question my choice of going there alone. A reasonable person might have left by slowly backing away. Unfortunately for me, my nosy side dwarfed any reason I possessed. I couldn't walk away until I knew the reason for the argument.

"Your step-dad seems like a jerk. What's his deal, anyway?"

Chris took a deep breath and tried calming down before responding. "He put me in charge of this truck, and I think I've done a great job. Business is booming. We're making great money."

"If that's all true, what's the problem?" I asked. If the truck was making money, you'd think his step-dad would be happy. Apparently, that wasn't the case.

"We need more help. With the number of customers we have daily, it's too much for two people to handle. All I wanted him to do was hire another person. That's all."

"Seems reasonable enough," I said. The Burger She Wrote truck experienced only half the business of his truck, and we had more than we could handle. I couldn't imagine how he managed to stay sane.

"He's too much of a tightwad, and doesn't care about anyone but himself. I'll never understand what my mom sees in him."

I shrugged my shoulders in response, but knew the answer to that by the car he was driving. It certainly wasn't his looks or charm. Let me give you a hint. It's green and rhymes with honey.

He continued. "If it weren't for him, I'd own three food trucks by now. He's only holding me back."

I grinned nervously and tried to lighten the mood, "Family, right?"

At this point, I felt awkward and wanted to head back. I needed an out.

"OK, Star, I'll be right there," I randomly shouted back in the direction of my truck.

Chris looked confused. "What's that? I didn't hear anything."

"That was Star. She gets impatient when I leave her alone," I said as I began to walk away. "It was good talking to you. See you around."

"Thanks for stopping by. Tell Star to give me a call sometime. We had a fun date a few weeks back."

I couldn't help but smile. "I'll let her know."

Once I returned to my truck, Star was waiting by the door for me.

"Did he ask about me?"

"Why would you care? I thought you didn't like him. What happened to ghosting him?"

"The beauty of the ghosting method is that it leaves the door open. It gives you the option to reappear in their lives if you change your mind."

When it came to dating, I knew very little. However, there was one thing I knew. Councilman Harmon was making a lot of enemies around Grove Park.

❧

5

The next morning started out like any other. That was until I reached Grove Park.

The sky was lit up like the fourth of July, which was odd given that it was only June 3rd. The usual smell of orange blossoms and ocean air was replaced by smoke fumes.

The fire was burning brightly in the spot that used to be the home of the Mama Mia food truck. All the spectators could do was watch from behind the yellow caution tape, as the Sunny Shores fire department worked hard to contain the blaze. It was a far cry from the usually drama-free morning in our small beachside town.

As soon as I spotted Chief Martin, I ran to him so he

could clue me in to what was going on. He was talking to other members of the police force and instructing them on where they needed to be. This was surely the most action any of them had seen in quite a while.

Our eyes made contact the moment I confronted him. I could see the worry and concern written all over his face.

"What's going on, Sam?"

"We received the call about a half-hour ago. The eyewitness said they heard a loud explosion inside Grove Park." He shook his head in disbelief of the situation at hand. "It appears to have been a propane explosion from inside Harmon's food truck."

"Oh no!" I exclaimed. "Was anyone inside?"

The Mama Mia food truck was a one man operation run by Chris Kelly. Chris Kelly was the biological son of Missy Harmon and step-son of John Harmon. While John was the full owner of the truck, Chris was in charge of all the day-to-day operations.

Chris seemed shy and a bit reserved, although he was always friendly to me. He would always wave or say hello each morning. I believe he was a bit stand-offish due to the controversy surrounding the parking space lottery. Even though it wasn't his call, a few of the food truck owners resented him for it.

As I watched the local volunteer firemen put out the smoky blaze, I hoped and prayed that Chris wasn't trapped inside the truck. It would have been a terrible and gruesome way to die.

Before I could ask Chief Martin if Chris was inside, I heard the screeching tires of a black Ford F-150 as it shot into the parking lot beside us. The door swung open and Chris Kelly hopped out of the cab and began to run towards the police barrier with a look of horror in his eyes.

"Easy there, son," Chief Martin said as he reached out his arm to hold Chris at bay. "You need to stay back. It's not safe right now."

"That's my truck," Chris screamed.

"I know it's a terrible feeling to have to watch your belongings being destroyed in front of you, but you have to stay back until the firemen are finished. For all we know, there could be another propane tank inside that is still intact."

"Oh, no!" Chris said as he put his hand on his head. "He's probably inside."

"What are you talking about?" Chief Martin asked. "Who's inside?"

Chris kept speaking frantically under his breath as he paced in a small circle. "I told him to wait on me. He doesn't know anything about running a food truck. Why did he want to meet here anyway? What did he do?"

"Chris, calm down and tell us who you're talking about," I said, trying to settle him down. "Who do you think was in the truck?"

Chris took a deep breath. "I think it's my step-dad, John Harmon."

6

"Councilman John Harmon?" Chief Martin asked. "Are you sure?"

Initially, I had my doubts. Other than the day prior, I had not seen John Harmon in Grove Park that summer. Before I saw him argue with his stepson Chris, I knew very little about John.

"He sent me a text early this morning to meet him here," Chris explained. "That's his car over there."

Chris pointed over to the parking lot. John Harmon's black BMW was parked in the distance with no sign of John around.

"Did it seem unusual to you for him to contact you like that?" I asked Chris, trying to make sense of the situation. "Do you think he was in some type of trouble?"

The police chief interjected. "Kara, this is a police investigation. Please step aside. I'll ask the questions."

"Now Chris... Do you think John was in some type of trouble?"

"Sure, it's odd for John to want to meet at the food truck, but I didn't think anything of it. I thought it was just another one of his drunken text messages."

"Since you seem sure that it might be him, I should call your mother. We may need you two to identify the body, or what's left of it."

Chris nodded his head in agreement. "I understand, but I should be the one to call Mom."

Chris pulled his phone out from his back pocket and began to dial. As he walked off, we both turned in the other direction to give Chris privacy.

"Kara, you should go home now. I appreciate your concern on the matter and how you want to help, but there's nothing you can do at this point," Sam said with a stressed and concerned look on his face. "I'm going to keep Grove Park closed today."

"Star, wake up. The craziest thing just happened," I said as I walked out of Grove Park and headed in the direction of downtown.

Star responded after letting out a big yawn. "What's up?"

"There's been an explosion at Grove Park. The police closed the entire park for the day."

"So you're saying that we're off today?"

"I guess that's one way to look at that, but you wouldn't believe—"

Before I could finish the sentence, Star interrupted me. "I'm going back to bed. Later."

As I heard the click on the other end, it was obvious Star was more interested in getting her Z's than hearing about what happened at Grove Park that morning. She wasn't the slightest bit interested.

I, on the other hand, could not stop thinking about it. It would have been the wise thing to do to go home and go to bed. Lord knows I needed more sleep, but my mind was traveling a thousand miles an hour. Rest was not in the forecast for me.

There was only one place I could go to help fuel the curiosity fire burning inside of me. I needed to talk to the one person whose curiosity and nosiness rivaled my own. That person was Bonnie May Calloway.

The Breezy Bean Café was more crowded than usual for a Wednesday morning at 8 a.m. This was no doubt due to the incident at Grove Park. A few of the food truck owners and townspeople were there. With Grove Park closed, there was nothing else for them to do.

Even with her shop being as busy as it was, Bonnie May had plenty of time to walk over and gossip... I mean discuss the hot topic of the morning. After all, according to Bonnie May, a good Southern woman never discussed her weight or age, and never gossiped. This came as no surprise to anyone who knew Bonnie May.

"It's the talk of the town, dear," Bonnie May said as she refilled my coffee. "Everyone is speculating."

I wondered how everyone was aware of the news this quickly, since the explosion only took place a couple hours earlier. I guess news traveled fast in a small town like ours.

"Speculating about what?"

"Oh, it's definitely him, dear. There's no doubt in anyone's mind about that." She drew closer in and whispered to me, "The real question is who did it?"

"Who killed him?" I asked. It had not yet occurred to me that any foul play was involved.

"John Harmon made a lot of enemies around town. Truth be told, all we can do is speculate to our heart's content."

"Why do you say that?" I asked.

"Any evidence left would've been burnt to a crisp, alongside John Harmon."

"Chief Martin mentioned something about an eye-witness, but he didn't say who it was."

"Oh… The eye-witness," Bonnie May said mockingly as she began to chuckle. "The only person to see anything was that old coot Willie Wylan. You'd get a more credible testimony from one of the palm trees in the park."

Willie Wylan was another one of the interesting characters that had relocated to Sunny Shores during the time I was away at college. Willie was a tall and lanky older Jamaican man who worked as an artist in Grove Park.

Willie was a little out there, to say the least. I didn't know much about him or his background, but a lot of the townsfolk had a less than stellar opinion of him. He was often referred to as crazy or homeless, due to his unkempt appearance and wacky antics.

I liked to give Willie the benefit of the doubt because he was always cordial to me. He would always say hello every morning on his way to his usual spot. Plus, his art was incredible. It was nothing like the hacks you would see in many tourist traps drawing caricatures.

"Besides," Bonnie May continued as she wiped down the table in front of me. "It could have been a number of people. Heaven knows that park is full of convicts working there."

"Who are you talking about?" I asked, as her comment took me by surprise. "I wasn't aware of any criminals working at Grove Park."

"Carlos Martinez is one of them. Rumor is he served time before moving to Sunny Shores."

"Carlos? Are you sure?"

She looked up at me and stared. It was as if I'd insulted her. Bonnie May didn't appreciate my lack of faith in her sources.

"I have it on good authority. There's no doubt in my mind that it's true. You can't trust anyone in this town. Sunny Shores is a town of second chances and new beginnings. Unfortunately, some people never change."

"Aren't there any cameras in Grove Park?" I asked. I thought it reasonable to assume the busiest public area in the city to have security cameras.

"Nope. Not one camera in the entire park," Bonnie May replied. "The cheapness of our penny-pinching mayor strikes yet again."

It wasn't the first time I'd heard Bonnie May take a cheap shot at our mayor, and I was sure it wouldn't be the last. Bonnie May was also a member of the Sunny Shores city council alongside our mayor and John Harmon. From what I could gather, Bonnie May and Mayor Coltrane didn't see eye-to-eye on most issues.

"I could talk all day dear, but it's already getting crazy in here."

With Grove Park shut down, the Breezy Bean Café was going to be extremely busy. In fact, every shop and restaurant downtown would be hopping that day. As much as Bonnie May loved to gossip, she loved money more. She was going to take advantage of it.

"No problem, Bonnie May," I said as I stood up from the table. "I should probably get home and get some rest. It's a rare day off for me."

7

As I walked home from the Breezy Bean Café, my mind swirled as if it had a tornado of information inside it. The explosion at Grove Park shocked the town. Sunny Shores, while being populated with kooky citizens, existed as a relatively uneventful town. I couldn't recall an incident this outrageous happening as long as I'd lived there.

I needed to talk to someone really badly, but Ty worked that morning, busy with clients. So I called Star back, waking her up yet again.

As she picked up the phone, she let out a yawn before speaking. "I hope you have a good reason for waking me up. It's not very often I get to sleep in."

"My grandma always said that the early bird catches the worm," I said in a tone I was sure was too chipper for her. The combination of excitement and caffeine perked me up to a level I was sure was a 10 on the annoying scale.

"Did your grandmother always talk in clichés?"

"Not always, but grandmas know how to dish out useful advice."

Star sighed. "My grandmother slept with a pistol under her pillow."

"To teach people to leave her alone when trying to sleep."

"I can't stop thinking about the accident this morning. In fact, I question if it's even an accident to begin with. Something seems fishy."

"We are by the ocean. The air usually smells fishy."

"I'm being serious. My gut instinct is going crazy. It's too bad there are no security cameras posted inside Grove Park."

Star yawned again. "Why not check the security cameras I installed on the truck?"

"Wait a minute. You installed a camera on my truck?"

"Actually four cameras. One for each corner," she replied. "You don't remember? I asked you the other day if you wanted to meet to put a few cameras up. You nodded your head yes, so I took a few hundred bucks out of the register and purchased the cameras."

"It's funny, I don't remember noticing any money missing from the register."

"You are so bad with money," Star said as she laughed. "Here's an idea for you. Why don't you let the accountant working for you keep your books and worry more about chopping onions?" She had a point. I lacked money management and bookkeeping skills. Not my strong points.

"Do you think one of the cameras recorded the incident that morning?"

"It's possible," Star said. She waited a few seconds before responding further. "Camera three is at the southeast corner of the truck. The Mama Mia food truck should be located directly in the camera's line of sight."

"It's a shame the park is closed and off-limits today. The anticipation is killing me. I wish we could watch the tape now."

"There's no physical tape. The cameras are wi-fi enabled and upload all videos to the cloud."

Every time I heard the term the cloud, it tickled me. My mind imagined large clouds of data and words cluttering the skies above us. I was clueless to how it really worked, but liked to think my understanding was correct.

"I didn't install wi-fi on the Burger She Wrote truck. How are you connecting the cameras to the Internet?"

"I'm borrowing the signal from the Cover Your Buns truck. Surely they don't mind."

"Do they even know you're stealing their wi-fi?"

"Stealing is kind of harsh, don't you think? If you take advantage of your neighbor having a bright outside light to do things in your own yard, is that considered stealing?" she said, trying to plead her case. "The important thing here is that we can access the footage from anywhere."

"Can you come over to my house and pull up the video on my computer?"

At this point, I was sure Star realized I wasn't going to take no for an answer. She agreed. "I'll head over there now. The quicker I can get there, the quicker I can get back to bed."

As I walked down my street and approached the house, Star surprised me by already being there.

"How did you get here before I did?"

"Probably because I actually own a car."

As she walked into my home, Star looked around, examining each little detail. "Nice house. I never would have imagined you were a collector of such unusual and creepy knickknacks."

"Those clowns are not mine. In fact, I'd smash them all to pieces with a sledge hammer, if it were up to me. Unfortunately, those belong to my mom. I'm staying with her for the time being."

"Why are they all facing the wall?"

My mom's collection of clown statues and collectibles was displayed in every corner of our home. No matter where you stood in the house, it appeared as if they were always looking in your direction. I grew to hate clowns. I developed a phobia for them. To this day, I wouldn't step foot within a ten mile radius of a circus.

My phobia stemmed from a traumatic incident in my

childhood, or at least, it felt traumatic to me. I watched the movie IT, based on the Stephen King novel, when I was eight years old. I snuck in the living room one night when my parents were watching it, when I was supposed to be in bed asleep. I hid behind the couch and peeked out the side, so I could see the screen. Two eyes glued to the tube, while both hands were gripping Mr. Fluffy for dear life.

For the next few weeks, creepy clowns haunted my dreams. In fact, I didn't sleep with the lights off until I was fourteen years old. Even then, I needed a night light.

Did I mention I hate clowns?

"Where's your mom at?" Star asked as she continued to look around the house.

"She's away at a writer's conference in Miami, and won't be back until Sunday evening. So it's just me until then."

Star smiled. "You and the clowns."

Not funny.

Star and I took a seat at the dining room table. I handed her my laptop so she could access the video.

She quickly pecked the keyboard and in seconds, had the video feed up.

Watching a video feed for clues in real life paled in comparison to how Hollywood portrayed it. If we were in a movie, Star and I would be sitting inside a high-tech van on an exciting stakeout. Instead, we were hunched around my kitchen table staring at my sad excuse for a laptop.

Star logged on to the website where we could access the video feed. She pecked at the keyboard so quickly, my head spun. I'm glad someone knew what they were doing.

"Do you think it'll be there?"

"The camera uploads a file daily for each 24 hour period. Unless Kim Kardashian broke the Internet again, it should be there," she explained. "Each of the four cameras has a separate folder. Here is. Camera three, the one you're looking for."

She scrolled through the files with a flick of the mouse. I wonder how she could even read the file name with them going by so fast. My head continued to spin as I tried to watch.

"Bingo," she called out. "This is it. June 7."

With a double-click of the mouse, Star started the recording video feed. Although the video quality was decent, it was dark and rainy due to it being so early in the morning. The fact that Grove Park lacked adequate lighting made it worse. With that being said, it was better than nothing.

"Wow, this is exciting," Star said as she watched the video. Star never lacked sarcasm, but she had a point. Believe it or not, there wasn't much action taking place at 2 a.m. in Grove Park on a Wednesday.

"We need to speed this up, or we'll be here all night," Star said as she increased the speed to twenty times faster. "That's better."

As the minutes on the video fast forwarded, nothing happened. Three hundred dollars spent on this equipment. Three hundred dollars I didn't know I spent to begin with. My attitude changed to one of disappointment and discouragement.

"Wait. Stop the video," I shouted as I pointed at the laptop screen. "Look over in the corner. It's a white Mercedes Benz."

Star paused the video without hesitation. "Is that John Harmon's car?" she asked. We both continued to stare at the screen.

"Restart the video, but slow it back down," I said.

We sat and watched while a man opened the car door and stepped outside. Again, the video was dark and grainy, so the identity of the man could be questioned. Although, the size and profile of the man fit the description of John Harmon.

"What's he doing?" Star asked as we continued to glue our eyes to the screen.

The man was pacing in a circle in front of the Mama Mia food truck. He held his left hand up to his ear as he walked around.

Saying the man walked around gave him too much credit. He noticeably stumbled and swayed as he walked. If I didn't know any better, I'd have said he was drunk. John Harmon's reputation included him being notorious for drinking like a fish.

"I think he's talking on his cell phone." Grove Park offered spotty cell reception at best. I noticed my cell reception turning worse when I stood inside the truck. Maybe that was why the man paced outside.

"By the way he's acting, he should be calling an Uber or cab," Star replied.

A few minutes later, John Harmon walked into the

truck. "That has to be John Harmon. I'm convinced," I told Star. "What was he doing there so early? Where was Chris?"

The minutes continued to tick by as nothing happened on the video. "I'm bored again," Star said as she stood up from the table. She walked over to the fridge and opened it up. "Have anything good to eat? All this sleuthing works up an appetite."

I imagined Star weighed a hundred pounds soaking wet. For someone as slender as she was, she knew how to put away the food. Although I wasn't sure where she put it. No matter how much she ate, Star failed to gain a pound. If I even looked at a potato chip, I gained a pound or two.

"Did you see that? I shouted.

Star turned around and muttered a few words with her mouth half-full of something. "See what?"

The screen displayed the Mama Mia food truck, or what used to be the Mama Mia food truck, set ablaze. The camera's resolution was perfect at that point. The fire shone so bright that it lit the park up like it was noon.

"Crap. I missed the explosion. I'm going to play it

back. You have any popcorn?" Star asked. "Now it's getting exciting."

Star sat back down and replayed the prior minute's footage. It was quite a sight to see the park go from quiet and peaceful to up in flames in a split second. I started to lose count of how many times she replayed it.

"Boom," she called out as we watched the truck explode for the umpteenth time.

"Can this thing play in slow-motion as well?"

"It sure can. Great idea," Star said. There was no doubt Star wanted to see the pure epic wonder of the explosion slowed down, but I had other ideas. The incident happened so fast. I wanted to be sure we didn't miss anything.

"That's it," I called out as I jumped out of my chair. "Look behind the truck, on the left hand side. There's someone back there walking towards the truck."

Dressed from head-to-toe in black, a mysterious figure appeared from behind a palmetto tree. Walking towards the truck, the man carried a large metallic object in his right hand. A slight reflection of light shone off the object as the man swung it back and forth.

"Is that a propane tank?" Star asked. It indeed appeared to be a propane tank. Having an extra propane tank on site helped explain the massive explosion that eventually took place.

"Where did he go?" I asked as the mysterious person in black disappeared behind the Mama Mia truck.

I waited only briefly for my question to be answered. The unidentified figure appeared to walk out from behind the truck, noticeably without the object he carried over there in the beginning. He looked around briefly, then ran away as quick as he could. A moment later, the truck went boom.

"He sure bolted out of there in a hurry," Star said while still munching on my food.

"Don't you understand what this means?" I asked Star as my heart began to race with excitement.

"Don't play with fire."

"Well, yes, that too, I guess," I responded as Star's quip derailed my thought. She had a knack for that. "This means the explosion wasn't an accident. Someone murdered John Harmon."

"What now?" Star asked.

"I know just the man to take this to."

8

I f there was anyone in Sunny Shores I could trust besides my mother, Sam Martin was the one. Sam Martin held the office of the Sunny Shores Police Chief. I grew up knowing Sam as my father's partner on the force. The two of them were detectives on the police force for almost fifteen years. Because of him and my father being so close, I thought of him as a member of my own family.

Star dropped me off at the Sunny Shores Police Department before going back home. As I walked through the large glass double doors, I felt a sense of calm and comfort. Being inside those walls, I felt as if I was home. I loved when my father took me to the police station. I blamed him for my love affair with the law and mysteries in general.

The feeling of being inside the police station turned bittersweet as the thought of my father entered my mind. To keep my heart from sinking further, I avoided looking in the direction of where his desk sat. There were too many fond memories of sitting in his chair, pretending to be a detective.

"Kara," a sweet, soft voice sounded out from behind. "It's so good to see you."

I turned to see a familiar face: Officer Janet Moses. Janet's job was to work the front desk and phones for the Sunny Shores police. She had worked there for as long as I could remember. Her smile brightened my mood as it was always contagious.

"How have you been?" I asked as we both reached for a hug. "It's been too long."

"I know. I felt bad that I didn't get to talk to you much at the funeral. You handled it well, Kara. You father was a great man. I'm so sorry for your loss. He is truly missed around here."

I took a deep breath. No matter how many times his name had come up in conversations, I still felt sadness every time someone mentioned him. I hoped it would get better with time.

"Thank you, Janet," I replied. "Is Sam around? I need

to show him something in regard to the incident and Grove Park this morning."

"He's in his office. I'll walk you over there."

As we walked to Sam's office, I tried to run through what I would say in my head. Doing something like this was new to me. I wasn't completely sure what to do, but I knew something had to be done.

"What are you doing here?" Sam asked as he greeted us at the door. Janet walked away and he led me into his office.

My mind was racing with too many thoughts at once, so I blurted out the first thing that popped into my head.

"It was John Harmon," I shouted.

"What are you talking about?" he asked as he stared at me in confusion.

"John Harmon was the one who burned in the truck."

"We know that already."

"That's not all," I said as I pulled out my cell phone from my purse. "The explosion wasn't an accident."

"What are you trying to say?" Sam asked. "It seems

reasonable when someone inexperienced messes with propane."

"That's not what happened," I replied sternly. "John Harmon was murdered."

"Kara, I appreciate your enthusiasm. I really do. It reminds me of how your father was," Sam said. "But I told you the police would handle it. At this point, the case is considered closed. There's no reason for further investigation."

"I understand, but I have evidence that clearly shows that it wasn't an accident."

"Evidence?"

"Star installed four security cameras on my truck. One was pointed in the direction of John Harmon's truck. See for yourself."

I opened the video that Star saved on my phone. I played the entire incident as Sam watched from his chair. His face looked more serious as each second went by.

"Hmm…"

Sam stood up and walked behind me and closed his office door. He took a deep breath as he walked back over to his desk.

"You have to understand the position that the mayor has put me in. Tourism is the only thing that's keeping this town alive financially."

I was confused at his response. "What does that have to do with anything? This man was murdered."

"I know it's hard for you to understand, but we don't want to end up with the same situation that happened to Parrot Bay. Since the orange juice factory closed, tourism is all this town has. Without it, we would be bankrupt."

"But I have evidence. The video clearly shows a man in black carrying a propane tank to the truck and going inside."

"Your video doesn't clearly prove anything. The person in black could be a man or woman. There is nothing in that video that could match it to any one person. It proves nothing."

I felt flabbergasted. The Sam Martin I grew up knowing wouldn't dismiss strong evidence such as this. He would at least look it over and sleep on it. For some reason I couldn't understand, he'd dismissed me completely.

"Why are you so interested in this case, Kara? This is about your father, isn't it?"

"Maybe so…"

"Your father wasn't only my partner, but my best friend as well. He was like a brother to me."

"I know, but…"

"Kara, you have to believe me. I did everything in my power to find your father's killer. I spent long hours and late nights going through his case file, but there just wasn't enough evidence to identify the person behind it."

"I believe you, but why are you ignoring the evidence in this case?"

"The mayor has cut my funding, and I have limited resources. He's directed us to close this case and focus on more important things."

"Like what?"

He stood in front of me, clueless and without a good response. He appeared conflicted.

"If additional evidence was found that could tie the murder to a particular person, the department would be forced to reopen the case," he said as he took a deep breath. "But until then, the case is closed."

As I left his office, one thought dominated my mind. If something needed to be done to bring the true murderer to justice, the police weren't going to do it.

I knew I would have to investigate it myself.

9

As I sliced tomatoes the next morning inside my truck, my mind was focused on the death of John Harmon. No matter what anyone said, I was convinced without a shadow of a doubt that it was no accident. Someone was out for blood, and I wanted to get to the bottom of it.

A steady stream of questions flowed through my head, like a rushing river. I needed answers, or I'd drive myself insane. So I decided to go straight to the source. Since I couldn't interview the victim for obvious reasons, I'd have to interview the next best option, an eye-witness.

Only one person in town was an eye-witness to the incident, and that was Ol' Willie Wylan.

Willie was an older Jamaican gentleman. He'd moved to Sunny Shores during the period that I was away at college, so I knew very little about him. He was tall, lanky, and had long, charcoal grey dreadlocks.

His attire left little to be desired. Willie wore the same off-white dingy Tommy Bahama shirt with cut off jean shorts every day. If you didn't know any better, you would mistake him for a homeless person. At least, I didn't think he was homeless.

Regardless of his unkempt appearance, Willie was cordial each time I encountered him. Willie never missed an opportunity to say hello. With his loud, thick Jamaican accent, he stood out.

Putting my prep work aside, I decided to walk over to the boardwalk area to try to catch Willie.

Although most of the citizens described him as loony, Willie was an extraordinary artist. He painted portraits for tourists strolling by. Most days, Willie set himself up on the boardwalk. He only required a wooden stool, his paint, brushes, canvas, and an easel.

As I walked along the boardwalk, many of the vendors in town were setting up their booths. Like most mornings, Willie was sitting on his stool, painting. You couldn't miss him if you tried. He was smiling and singing "Under the Sea." As he painted, he rocked back and forth, dancing to his own melody.

"Ahh, Miss Kara," Willie said as he flashed a big smile across his face. He had a beautiful smile, if you didn't mind the fact that half of his teeth were missing. "Wonderful morning to ya, dear."

"Good morning, Willie," I replied. He continued to sway back and forth, stroking his brush across the canvas. "What are you painting?"

You couldn't have asked for a more gorgeous morning overlooking the Atlantic Ocean. The sun rising over the ocean shone a beautiful shade of orange. My first thought was that he was painting this picture-perfect sunrise.

I should've known better.

"It be a chicken ridin' a turtle," Willie said, laughing, as he picked up the canvas and turned it around for me to see.

"It certainly is…" I said as I stared at his painting.

"What can I do for ya?" he asked as he picked up his

paint brush. "Would ya like a painting of yourself? No charge."

"That's very sweet of you, but I'll have to take a rain-check."

"Very well. All you youngins only want self-sees with ya cell phones nowadays."

I laughed. "I think you mean selfies, Willie."

"Selfies or self-sees, doesn't matter, dear," he replied, shaking his head. "Dem devices gonna put Ol' Willie out of business."

"I've seen your work, and I highly doubt that'll happen anytime soon. What I really came here for was to ask you about the other morning. Chief Martin said you were the only one to witness the explosion."

"Dat's right," Willie said as he put his paint brush down and stood up. "I be taking my mornin' walk, I tell ya. Then it happened."

"What?"

"Dat truck went BOOM, I tell ya. BOOM!" he said as he gestured wildly with his arms.

"Did you see anyone else, or anything unusual besides that?"

"I did see a man dressed in all black runnin' like da wind out of Grove Park."

"Really?" I asked as my ears perked up. Finally, it was a lead. "Are you sure it was a man?"

"I couldn't see his face clearly, but I'm positive it be a man. He be havin' a lime green ski mask on, but took it off while he be runnin'," he said in a very convincing and matter-of-fact tone. "I tell ya, that fella was runnin' nonstop. I be out of breath just watchin' him."

"Did you tell the police?"

"I told that fella, Martin, the police chief," Willie explained. "But he not be interested in what Ol' Willie be sayin'."

"Hmm… That's interesting."

"I'll tell ya, somethin' smell mighty fishy in dis town, and it ain't da low tide."

Willie's story was captivating. I almost lost track of time until I glanced down at my watch. It was almost 9:30 a.m., and I needed to get back to work.

"I better get back to the truck, and start prepping for the day," I said. "Thank you, Willie. This was a big help."

As I walked away, I began to realize that Willie's story confirmed my suspicions all along. The murder wasn't an accident. John Harmon's goose was cooked on purpose. Not only was there video evidence, but an eye-witness account.

A new question began to burn inside me. Why did Chief Martin blow off Willie's story?

"One more thing, dearie," Willie shouted as I was walking away.

I stopped quick and turned around to see what he wanted.

"What's that?"

"Dis town be full of crooks from top to bottom. Be careful who you be trustin'."

As I walked back to the Burger She Wrote truck, Willie's words pierced through me like a sharp knife of truth.

Was there anyone I could truly trust? At this point, I wasn't sure.

∾

"I've been up most of the night thinking about this case," I said.

"Slow down, Speedy Gonzales. How many cups of coffee have you had this morning?"

I walked over to the dry erase board used to display our daily menu and wiped it clean. Ty's jaw dropped as I erased the menu of the day that was just completed.

"Are you kidding me?" Ty said as he watched me clear off the dry erase board with a few quick swipes. "That took a lot of time to write out. I don't even remember it all now."

"It's not that hard to remember," I pointed out. I called out the entire menu by heart. The look on Ty's face didn't show him being impressed.

"I understand you have your freakish photographic memory, but did you not realize that the board has a back side?" Ty explained as he flipped the white board over.

"Anyway, to get back to the subject at hand," I replied. "It looks like we have ourselves an old-fashioned mystery."

Being a fan of mystery books and television shows growing up, it didn't take much to get me excited about the prospect of solving my very own mystery. So I picked up the dry erase marker and began to scribble on the whiteboard.

"Everyone knows the first step to solving a mystery is to figure out who the suspects are," I said.

Ty sarcastically replied, "Sure, Kara, everyone knows that."

"Obviously," Star replied, mockingly, as they both laughed.

"I'm serious, you guys," I said. "Since the police aren't willing to do anything about this, it's up to us to solve this case."

"Why us? Who really cares about John Harmon?" asked Star. "He's a jerk."

"None of that matters," I said, taking a deep breath before continuing. "It's not right. If he was murdered, the killer should be brought to justice. His family or friends deserve closure."

I knew more than anyone the pain of losing a family member. On top of the pain of losing my father, a slew of unanswered questions surrounded his death.

Ty could sense how serious it was for me. Being my best friend since the third grade, he was the one person I could share anything with. I shared more about my father's death to him than to my ex-boyfriend. We had a special connection.

"We're just messing with you, Kara," Ty replied, as he put his hand on my shoulder. "If this means that much to you, I support you all the way. I'm here for you, as well as Star." He turned to her and said, "Isn't that right, Star?"

"I guess so," Star said, not appearing as convinced as Ty. "I'm on the clock for this, right?"

"Awesome. You both are in?" I smiled as I turned back towards the board. "On to the suspects…"

I drew a large number one on the board in lime green ink. The task at hand should've been finishing our prep work for the day. We needed to cut potatoes and change the fryer oil before opening. Those tasks were now on the back-burner and could wait.

I pressed the dry erase marker against the board and said, "Suspect number one is…"

"That gold-digging wife of his," Star said, interrupting my big reveal.

"Yep," Ty interjected, as he was quick to agree with Star. "There's no question about it."

"Missy Harmon it is," I said as I wrote her name down on the board.

1. Missy Harmon

Missy was suspect number one. To say Missy was unpopular around town would've been an understatement, to say the least. She was as well liked as a swarm of mosquitoes in summer. Although, she was likely more of a pest to the locals.

"Let's be real. There's no way a woman like her would be with him unless money were involved," said Star. "That marriage screamed of being a sham. She wasn't fooling no one."

Although Missy was our unanimous number one suspect, my intuition was sparked with an ounce of doubt. It almost seemed too obvious and cliché.

"If Missy's a suspect, you'd need to consider this person as well," Ty replied as he reached his hand out, wanting me to hand him the marker. "May I?"

Ty took the marker from my hands. I anxiously watched as he wrote the name down of suspect two.

It was a relief to see Ty actively participating in something that meant so much to me.

2. Chris.

"His stepson?"

"It's no secret that those two had issues," Ty explained. "Also, was it a coincidence that he was late to the park the day his step-father was murdered?"

"I want to play too," Star said as she ripped the marker out of Ty's hands. She went over to the board and wrote a name under Chris's.

3. Carlos

She stepped back and smiled. "That's the man who did it. It's obvious."

"Carlos?" I asked. "You really think he could have done it?"

"Don't get me wrong, he's been nice to me. You can't discount the evidence that surrounds him."

Star's point about Carlos possibly being the killer seemed valid. First, John Harmon stole Carlos's food truck location. Second, he ordered an extra propane tank.

10

There was just too much evidence to ignore. First of all, Carlos had been publicly outspoken when it came to Councilman Harmon. Everyone in town knew that Carlos was angry with him. Not only did he steal his spot, he caused Carlos's business to tank. Not to mention, he ordered an extra propane tank a day before the explosion.

Even worse, the rumors of him previously being in jail only added more fuel to the fire. Pardon my pun.

When I approached Carlos's food truck, he was inside chopping jalapenos. He already seemed angry —he was muttering something under his breath as he loudly sliced each pepper.

"Good morning, Carlos," I said as I knocked on the door. "Crazy couple days around here, huh?"

"You're telling me," Carlos said as he shook his head in agreement. He stopped chopping and lifted the knife in the air. "If you ask me, that gringo deserved it."

As he spoke, he kept shaking the knife. It made me a bit nervous, so I backed up just a bit.

"There's a lot of rumors going around town about who might have done it."

"Oh really," Carlos said as he placed the knife down on the counter. That caused me to breathe a sigh of relief. "He had a lot of enemies. I'm sure that there were more than a few to do him in eventually."

"He did have quite the reputation. Some names around Grove Park have been thrown around as potential murderers."

"You don't say," Carlos said as he chuckled a bit. "Next you'll tell me I'm one of them."

"To be honest, Carlos, some people think you did it."

"Wait, you're not one of those people, are you?"

"Of course not. I don't think you're capable of that. Although, there are a few suspicious things."

"What do you mean?"

"According to the propane delivery guy, you ordered an extra propane tank a day before the explosion happened."

"That's ridiculous," Carlos said. "The reason I ordered an extra tank is because I was hired to cook for the Swansons' family reunion."

"Oh…"

"Plus, I still have the tank out back," Carlos said as he started to walk out of the food truck. "Follow me and I'll show you."

I followed Carlos as we walked around to the back of his truck. Although I respected and admired Carlos, my mind questioned whether or I could trust him. Unfortunately, that trust continued to fade. The empty spot where the propane tanks were held didn't help.

"I don't understand," he shouted as he frantically looked around. "I left the tank right here, in this spot."

"You didn't have it locked up?" I asked.

"No, I never had a reason to before."

I found it strange that Carlos would leave a full propane tank outside his truck in the open. The first thing I was told when I ordered propane was to keep it locked up. My friend Len insisted on it before he would even deliver.

"Don't worry about it, Carlos. I'm sure it'll turn up," I said to help ease his nerves. I noticed him getting angrier by the second. I knew he had blood pressure issues. The last thing I wanted to do was cause him to have a stroke.

"You don't think I'm capable of murdering John Harmon? Do you?"

"Not exactly."

"What does that mean?" he said as he became more defensive. His face turned red and he tapped his foot.

As usual when I'm nervous, I began to talk at light-speed. "It's just that you were so angry at him the other day. Plus, the missing propane tank, and how you were in jail…"

As soon as I muttered that last line, I knew I went too far. I had no intention to blurt that last fact out. It wasn't uncommon for my mouth to outrun my mind.

"Who told you that?" he said as his voice rose.

"I didn't mean to offend, but I heard…"

"You don't have any idea what you're talking about. You need to leave. Now!"

Carlos turned away and walked back to his truck. A loud thud echoed through Grove Park as he slammed the door behind him. I had no intention of getting him angry, but what I'd said had touched a nerve. The last thing I wanted to do was stick around and find out what happened next.

11

Cooking and preparing dishes had a calming effect on me. After the confrontation with Carlos, I needed it. Focusing on preparing the menu for the day helped take my mind off it.

You wouldn't think a burger food truck would require much work, but you'd be surprised. All of our ingredients were fresh. After finishing the desserts, we would spend the morning patting fresh hamburger patties, chopping lettuce, slicing tomatoes, and everything else that took part in making the perfect burger.

My real secret was the meat. Instead of sprinkling the garlic, salt, and pepper on the outside of the patty, I would mix the patty up. This way, the spices mixed throughout the hamburger patty. I would pat out enough patties to last until dinner.

Star would do various prep jobs while I patted out the meat. She was an efficient worker, but couldn't stay quiet for more than a minute. She loved to give me life advice, which was funny coming from someone four years younger.

"So tell me about his ex-boyfriend of yours. Why did he break up with you?"

"I'd rather not talk about it, Star. But I broke up with him."

"Then why do you still take his calls?"

"Dustin and I were together for eight years. It's hard to just turn it off, like it's a light switch."

With impeccable timing, as usual, my phone rang. Sure enough, it was Dustin calling again. Before I could answer the phone, Star interfered.

"He's your ex for a reason," Star exclaimed as she wrestled the phone away from my hands.

"I know, Star," I said as I continued to struggle to take back my phone. "Something might be wrong. He may need my help."

"Doesn't matter now," she said sternly. "I'm doing this for your own good."

Without a moment's notice, Star threw my phone out of the front window of the food truck. It flew about a hundred feet and bounced before settling in the grassy quad in the center of the parking lot.

For a split second, I was more impressed than mad. Star had quite the arm on her. Maybe she was in the wrong line of work. Those thoughts suddenly faded when I realized she'd chucked an eight-hundred dollar electronic device I was still making payments on.

"What the heck?" I screamed at her. "Do you realize how much that phone cost?

"Relax, Kara. Your phone insurance will pay for it," she said as she put her arm on my shoulder. "You purchased the insurance on your phone, right?

I didn't respond, but turned my head away from her. I tried avoiding eye contact with her, especially when I knew she was right.

"You were too cheap to pay the extra ten bucks a month for insurance?"

"That's beside the point, Star."

She shook her head in agreement and said, "You're right. Instead of focusing on some creep from the past, you should look forward and notice what's in front of you. More specifically, that dark-haired hunk walking this way."

The 6'2" handsome hunk she referred to was one of the co-owners of the Cover Your Buns hot dog truck. Both owners were new to Sunny Shore, so I knew little about them. They both seemed friendly, not to mention handsome.

"I think one of you may have dropped this," the hunk said as he placed my phone on the counter in front of us.

"Thank you so much," I said. "It slipped out of my friend's hand."

He laughed. "That was quite a slip."

"I'm Will," he said. "I'm not sure we've been properly introduced."

"I'm Kara, and this is Star."

"I feel bad for not stopping by earlier, but we've been swamped trying to get this new business off the ground."

"I can totally relate," I said, still smiling like a school girl. "So what do you think of our little town so far?"

"I've been in town a few weeks, but haven't ventured out much."

"That's too bad," I said as I twisted my hair around my finger. "You need to get out. Sunny Shores has some very quaint, but nice restaurants."

"So I've heard," he replied. "I hate going alone. It would be nice to have someone show me around who knows their way around town."

"That's true," I replied.

Star couldn't take it anymore. So she blurted out, "He's asking you out, dummy."

If I wasn't nervous enough, Star just made it ten times worse. I had no idea what to do. So I tried to play it off. "That's sweet of you, but things are so crazy right now…"

"Don't say another word, I understand," Will said as he grabbed the pen from the counter. He scribbled something on a piece of paper and handed it to me.

Will Stark 239-555-8715

"Here's my number if you change your mind. No pressure at all."

As Will walked away, Star punched me on the arm and said," Are you an idiot? That dude is hot. Why are you so afraid of moving on?"

If I had a nickel for each time someone asked about my dating life, I would be able to afford my dream restaurant. I didn't, so the food truck was all I could afford.

"Star, I don't think I'm ready to get back out there yet." My undivided attention was focused on growing my business. I didn't have time to worry about men. The last thing I wanted to do was dive head-first back into the dating pool.

"Go to dinner with him as friends. What do you have to lose? You'll get a free meal out of the deal. Plus, it'll help get your mind off work and more importantly, Dusty."

"Dustin."

"Whatever. If you don't do it, I will."

"He is cute."

"So what's the problem? Just do it."

"Alright, I'll go with him. But get one thing straight, it's not a date."

Star smiled. "Are you trying to convince me or yourself?"

"Hey Will!" I screamed, trying to get his attention as he walked back to his truck. He turned around and flashed a smile. It was almost as if he knew I'd changed my mind.

"On second thought, a friendly dinner would be nice."

"Great! How does Thursday night work for you? We could meet at Pelican Pete's around 9 p.m."

I looked over at Star. She was nodding her head up and down while staring me in the eyes. I was sure she was laughing inside over my awkwardness.

"Sounds good."

"Awesome. Can't wait."

I tried to stay cool, calm, and collected. "Never let them see you sweat," as Bonnie May would say. Unfortunately, I was the complete opposite of cool, so I said the first thing that entered my mind.

"It's a date."

꩜

12

"Did you hear that?" I asked Star. I heard a slight noise coming from the back door of the truck.

"Hear what?" Star asked, as she continued to wash dishes in the sink.

"That noise coming from the back of the truck. It sounds like someone trying to get in."

"I didn't hear a thing. Are you sure you're not being overly paranoid? Maybe your mind's playing tricks on you?"

"Maybe so," I said as I shrugged my shoulders. With my mother out of town on business, I had the house to myself. Due to my tendency of being a big chicken, I lacked a good night's sleep.

"There it is again," I shouted. I heard something for sure that time. "Turn the water off and stay still."

Star sighed out of frustration, but obliged with my request. She turned off the water and dried her hands. "What now?"

"Shh," I whispered, motioning for her to come over and stand by me. We stood perfectly still, not making a peep.

"Did you hear it that time?" The sound of something scratching the door echoed through the truck. Someone or something had tried getting it.

"It's nothing," Star said as she left my side. She walked slowly towards the back door, tip-toeing softly. The sound of scratching and clawing increased with each step Star took.

"Are you crazy?" I asked her. I reached over and picked up the first object I could get from the counter. If someone tried something, I'd mess them up real good with the wooden mixing spoon I picked up.

"I feel like we're in the opening scene of a horror movie," I said nervously. "And you know how those turn out."

"Overreact, much?" Star giggled as she reached out

her hand and opened the door. Lacking any hope of successfully defending myself, I closed my eyes.

Meow.

"It's just Mr. Whiskers," Star said. Star reached down and picked the cat up.

"Are you feeding that stray cat again?"

"He's so sweet," Star said. She opened the door of the truck, bent down, and began to pet the cat. "Come on, Kara. Just listen to him purr."

I couldn't lie… The cat was adorable. I often wondered why he didn't have a home.

"Why don't you just take him home with you?" I asked. "I don't think anyone would stop you from adopting him."

"I wish. I would take him in a heartbeat," she said, as she continued to pet him. "My landlord doesn't allow pets."

"Be careful not to let him in. We can't have a stray cat spray his germs inside the truck. The health inspector would shut us down for sure. She's not a fan."

"Knock Knock," a voice called out.

When I noticed who it was, I sprung out of the van and ran outside to greet him with a big hug.

"It's so good to see you. I've missed you," I said as I placed my arms around his neck.

That familiar voice was none other than Kyle Harris. Kyle was a childhood friend of mine who lived two houses down from me. It was not uncommon for Kyle, Ty, and I to play outside until after dark every night, at least until our moms called for us to come inside from the back porch.

I'd not seen him for a few years now, but he looked almost exactly the same. Kyle was tall and skinny, with dark thick framed glasses. He wore that type of glasses well before hipsters made them cool.

Kyle's father, Harold Harris, owned Sunny Shores Insurance and Trust. If you needed car, homeown-er's, life, or any other type of insurance, it was the place to go. With Kyle's father not aging too well, Kyle took over the day-to-day operations of the business.

"How's the food truck business?" he said as he stepped back and examined the outside of my truck. "Burger She Wrote, eh? That's hilarious."

One of the many games we played as kids included

pretending to be sleuths. Kyle, Ty, and I would run around the neighborhood solving imaginary crimes we concocted in our minds. We weren't too original though, because most of our ideas came from Encyclopedia Brown novels and Scooby Doo cartoons.

"So, have you solved the case of John Harmon's murder?"

"Who, me? Why would you think I'd be interested in doing that?"

Kyle pointed to the name decal on my truck. "Really?" Where would I ever get such an idea?"

I tried to hold back a grin, but was unsuccessful. "Fair enough. You caught me."

That's one of the great things about friendship. Whether you consider it a blessing or a curse, a true friend can look through your B.S. and get to the truth.

Kyle took a sip of his cherry limeade and said, "It's a good thing Mrs. Harmon doubled John's life insurance policy last month. She should be set for life."

My ears turned up and I did a double-take to make sure I heard him correctly.

"Are you saying Missy increased her husband's life

insurance policy recently? As in right before his murder?"

Kyle slapped his right hand on his forehead. "I probably should have kept that bit of info to myself."

"Probably," I said as I shook my head in agreement. "However, you could look at it another way. One could argue that nugget of information is important evidence that shouldn't be ignored."

"True," he said, as he looked around nervously. It was as if he wanted to make sure no one was listening.

I couldn't blame him for being careful. Who knew who might listen? In fact, my truck could have been bugged. Star installed the camera system without me knowing. There was no telling what else she could have done.

He reached his head over the counter and whispered, "A large majority of his estate was already tied up to another beneficiary. It was in her best interest to take out a large policy on her husband, especially if she wanted to continue the same lifestyle after his death."

"Another beneficiary, are you sure?"

"I'm one-hundred percent positive, Kara."

He glanced at his watch and realized he lost track of the time.

"I've got to run. My next appointment is in ten minutes."

As Kyle walked away, Star returned from the store and entered the truck.

"Who was that?" she said. "Another nerdy friend of yours?"

"Nerdy friends? What are you trying to say?"

"It's not an insult," Star explained as she placed the grocery bags on the counter. "Being nerdy is in nowadays."

I laughed. "That's good to know."

"Besides, he's kinda cute."

13

Before Star allowed me to have dinner that night with Will, she insisted that I do something with my hair. As much as I protested the thought of going to the beauty salon, Star wouldn't take 'no' for an answer. So I made an appointment to the only beauty salon I knew in town.

Cookie Pearson owned Cookie's Beauty Salon located on Dune Drive, a mile east of downtown. I remembered Cookie's Salon from as long back as childhood. My mother visited her shop a few times a year to get her perm, back when perms were a thing.

I grew up a tomboy, so I hated going with my mother to the beauty shop. So much, in fact, that I brought my Walkman and listened to music the entire time.

Even then, the music wasn't enough to drown out the constant gossiping and bickering.

I preferred going with my father to Pappy's Barbershop. I received my hair cuts there growing up. It drove my mother nuts. My dad found it hilarious, though.

I wasn't trying to be rebellious. Pappy's atmosphere was more laid back and relaxed. Although the men would mainly talk sports, they were known to gossip as well. At least the men were light-hearted in their gossiping, unlike the women, who sounded petty and jealous.

"Look everyone, little Kara Summers is back," Cookie called out as Star and I entered the shop. I intended to slip in quietly, but the loud cowbell attached to the doorknob thought otherwise.

"Have a seat over there, dear," she said as she pointed to a set of empty chairs in the corner. "I'll be with you in a bit."

"Like I was saying," Cookie said as she continued the conversation we'd interrupted. "She's been strutting around town like her... you know what... doesn't stink."

Cookie was talking as she took the rollers out of Ms.

Tara Holmes's hair. Apparently, perms still were a thing in Sunny Shores after all. I missed the memo on that one.

Tara Holmes's late husband, Barney, owned the site that the old Sunny Shores orange juice factory sat on. After his passing, Tara tried selling the land, which was prime real estate close to the beach. A group of investors planned to build a resort in the area. Unfortunately for her, and her pocketbook, the town council voted against it.

"I don't think I've seen her wear black once," Tara interjected. "I don't know how they do things in Tampa, but we have class here in Sunny Shores. I don't know who she thinks she is."

"Yep," Cookie replied. "You can take away the trailer, but you can never remove the trailer trash."

"I know that's right," Tara replied.

"Seems a little harsh," Star said. Star liked playing devil's advocate and stirring the pot. She wasn't defending Missy Harmon. She couldn't have cared less. "People grieve in different ways. We don't know what lies inside her."

"Or whom…" Tara said as she began to giggle.

Cookie let out an audible groan. "That's awful, Tara. You shouldn't talk that way around these young girls."

Star smiled. "Kara's not that young."

"Do you really believe Missy cheated on John?" I asked while ignoring Star's comment.

"Rumors of her adulteress acts started from the day her tacky high heels touched the ground in Sunny Shores," Cookie said. "In fact, I saw it with my very own eyes in the last week."

"No you didn't," Tara replied. "I think the fumes in here are getting to your head."

Cookie tapped her feet in frustration. "I certainly did," she said as she raised her voice.

"Where?"

"Do you remember when I needed to run to Lake City last week?"

"Yes."

"On my way back, I passed the Cozy Cove Motel," Cookie explained as she turned to me. "I like to slow down when I pass by, as a lot of seedy activities take place there. You never know what you'll see."

"What did you see?"

"I saw Missy Harmon and a young man, both walking into one of the rooms."

"Oh, really?" Tara said as she groaned. It was clear she doubted Cookie's story. "Who was this mysterious young man?"

"I couldn't tell. I only saw the back of him."

"How convenient," Tara said. "Are you sure you didn't stop by Jack's Liquor Store on the way there? "

"I did, but that's beside the point," Cookie said as she turned my way again. "I like to have a drink every now and again. Dr. Bill said it's good for the heart."

"I don't think he was referring to whisky."

"Oh hush." Cookie tapped her foot louder. "I'm telling you, Tara, it's the truth."

The bickering between Cookie and Tara began to give me a headache. I spoke up. I figured it was my only chance.

"If most of the town knew about Missy's transgressions, wouldn't John know as well?" I asked. "How could he not get sick of it after a while?"

"The councilman was anything but innocent

himself," Tara said. "John's habit of visiting strip clubs and spending thousands continued on after his marriage. Those two fought all the time. The relationship was toxic to say the least."

Cookie and Tara verified the information Bonnie May provided earlier.

"Those two made little effort to hide their issues. They were known to air their dirty laundry out in the open," Cookie said as she continued to style Tara's hair, if you could call it that.

"Just the other day, Hailey Hopkins stopped by for a trim. She and her husband Harold are neighbors of John and Missy. She told me she heard screaming and fighting coming from the Harmons's estate the other night. She contemplated calling the police because of how loud they were."

"Interesting," I replied. Finally, something substantial out of those two, I thought.

Star cut to the point. "So you think the hussy killed him?" Star said with a sarcastic tone, although they failed to pick it up.

"I'll tell you this. I don't believe for one minute it was an accident," Cookie responded as she pointed a hair-roller at Star. "I wouldn't put it past her."

"Who knows, really," Tara chimed in. "With the amount of enemies that man collected over the years, the killer could have been any number of people. His wife, step-son, mistress, or anyone in town with a pulse could have done it."

Cookie kicked the pedal on the chair and spun Tara around to face the mirror. "So what do you think?" Cookie asked as she revealed Tara's perm. Tara's hair looked like it was pulled out of the 1980's.

Star turned to me and whispered, "What is that thing on her head? A dead poodle?"

I tried to fight it, but failed. I snickered. "I think it's her hair."

Star looked up and stared at my hair and smirked. At first, I failed to understand her intent.

"What is it? Is there something in my hair?" I asked. I rubbed my fingers through to make sure.

Star didn't answer. Instead, she looked in the direction of Tara's hair and back to mine. After she repeated this a few times, I got the hint.

There was no way on earth that woman was getting close to touching my hair. I preferred my frumpy style to the act of torture Cookie performed on Tara's hair.

Without saying a word to each other, we both realized our only course of action. We had to split. Gathering our things quietly, we tiptoed toward the door. Cookie and Tara were engrossed in their argument, and wouldn't have a clue we left.

Wrong.

"Where are you two going?" Cookie asked. We were busted. "I'm done with Tara. You're up next."

I needed an out without hurting her feelings. So I did what any self-respecting Southern girl would do. I told a little fib.

"I'm sorry, Cookie. Food truck emergency. Maybe another time?"

"Just let me know, dear," Cookie said as she waved goodbye. "I'm pretty much open all month. It's strange. Bookings have been down lately."

I couldn't imagine why.

"So what now?" Star asked as we walked to her car. "I hoped we could do something about that hair of yours. Regardless of how much enjoyment I'd receive looking at you, even I couldn't let you do that to yourself."

"Thanks, I guess."

Dinner time was approaching. The Burger She Wrote truck needed a few more tasks completed before dinner time. Still, I wanted answers. I knew exactly where I needed to go next.

"If you don't mind, could you head back to Grove Park? I need you to start getting things ready for the dinner rush. I'll be along shortly."

"OK, but where do you need to go?"

I smiled. "It's time to pay an old friend a visit."

❦

14

"Pull over, right here," I yelled out loud as Star narrowly avoided missing my stop.

"My brake pads are almost worn to the metal since I've started giving you rides."

I'll admit that I stank at giving directions. My slow reaction time made matters worse. If it weren't for having a GPS in my ex's car, he would have dumped me years earlier.

"You're going to Pappy's Barbershop?" Star said, stunned. She thought about it for a moment, then shrugged her shoulders. "This place can't be any worse than Cookie's place."

I trusted Pappy and Pappy alone to cut my hair. This was the case since my father took me there as a little girl. I loved staring at the red and white striped barber sign out front. The sign reminded me of a lolly-pop. I gazed at it until I felt dizzy each time we visited.

When I walked up to the shop, I immediately spotted Pappy. He sat on the bench in front of the shop, reading the Sunny Shores Times. I stood still for a brief second and soaked it in. The moment and setting took me back to my childhood.

"Hey Pappy? Long time no see," I said.

Pappy folded the newspaper in two and placed it in his lap. He adjusted his glasses until his eyes were back in focus. As soon as he realized who I was, he grinned from ear to ear.

"Kara," he shouted as he jumped off the bench and give me a big squeeze. "It's about time you came by and see me. Once I heard you were back, I wondered when you'd come by."

"I wanted to come by sooner, but the truck has taken up most of my free time," I explained.

"Nonsense. Ol' Pappy knows how running your own business is. When I first started the barbershop, I spent the majority of the day here. I was gone so long my kids called the milk man daddy."

"Milk man? How old is this shop?" I asked as I laughed.

Pappy smiled. "Way too old, if you ask Mrs. Pappy. She's been wanting me to retire for years."

"Why don't you?"

"Have you met my wife?"

We both enjoyed a good laugh.

Pappy was a great man with an even better sense of humor. He was born in Cape Town, South Africa. His family emigrated to the United States when he was a boy. Pappy fought through poverty and racism as a young man, working hard and saving his money. By the time he was twenty-five, he saved enough to open his own shop.

"What can I do for you?"

I smiled. "Have time for a trim?"

"For you, always," he said as he opened the door for me. He invited me in and walked me to his barber chair.

My heart felt at ease from being inside those walls again. The place looked the same from the last time I visited. In the left corner, an old magazine rack stood.

It didn't contain a magazine from after 1990. He still had the glass lolly-pop case on the counter by the register. If I sat still enough, he'd give me an extra one.

If I closed my eyes, I could imagine my father sitting in the barber's chair. He laughed and cut up with the other men. They talked sports, politics, and occasionally women. They kept it clean when I was there.

"So just a trim, huh? Have a hot date?"

I hesitated for a moment before answering him. "Unfortunately, I do."

"You don't sound too excited," he said as grinned.

"It's nothing against the guy. He seems nice," I explained. "But a part of me feels like it's not ready to move on yet."

Pappy's demeanor and overall presence made people feel relaxed and open. The longer I was there, the safer I felt about sharing. To be honest, Pappy missed his calling in life. Instead of a barber, he should've been a psychiatrist.

"Well, Kara," he began as he pulled a fresh comb from the glass jar. "You gotta do what feels best for you. Don't worry about what others think."

His words rang true. The trait of trying to please others first described me perfectly. Not for lack of trying, I attempted to change. I liked pleasing people. It bothered me to think someone was upset with me.

"At least I can question Chris at the restaurant," I blurted out without thinking first.

With the sudden death of John Harmon, Missy allowed Chris to take over the day-to-day management of the restaurant. Since the Mama Mia food truck lay in rubble, Chris needed a new job. Quite frankly, it was a logical move.

"So, the rumors are true," he said as he began to trim my split ends. "Little Kara Summers, the private eye."

His response surprised me. "How did you know that?"

He chuckled. "This is a small town and word travels fast. Besides that, you're talking to a barber. Everyone spills the beans to me."

Everybody kept mentioning how small a town Sunny Shores was. I felt the town was shrunk daily by the way everyone knew my business. It made matters worse that discretion wasn't my strong suit.

"Your father became one of my best customers. In fact, I probably cut his hair more often than anyone else in town."

Hearing that made me smile. I almost forgot how often my dad visited Pappy for a haircut.

"And I tell ya, Kara, it wasn't because he liked his hair short."

"Then why?" I asked.

"Don't play coy with me. You are your daddy's daughter, that's for sure," he replied as he continued to cut my hair. "I bet you're here for the same reason he always came." He looked into the mirror, directly at my eyes. "You're looking for information on John Harmon's death, aren't you?

"I can't help it, Pappy. I possess this unquenchable thirst for solving this case. It's all I can think about."

He laughed. "Your daddy was the same way. He came here so often because he wanted to keep his ears to the street. Being a good investigator in a small town requires you blend in with the people. He was great at that."

"So what do you think happened to John Harmon?"

"Mr. Harmon was a rich and powerful man. He lived

a very successful life, and no one can deny that. However, to get to that point, he stepped on many folks along the way. Hurting others without remorse to get what he wanted led to a trail of victims. He amassed a lot of enemies."

"Who do you think could have done it?" I asked.

"A lot of the time in these cases, it all leads back to family."

"So you think someone in his family did it? Perhaps his wife or step-son?"

"Could be. You never know," he responded as he finished up. "I'll tell you this. My gut tells me it's not about money."

"Why so?" I asked.

"Blowing a person up with propane strikes me as a crime of passion or revenge. Someone wanted him to not just die, but suffer. If it were over money, I would imagine someone using a less gruesome means of murder."

His perspective was interesting and brought up a few good points. I had a lot more to think about. Maybe I was looking at the case in the wrong light.

"What do you think?" he asked as he rotated the

chair to face the mirror. "Simple and understated. My specialty."

"Looks great, Pappy. Thank you."

"My pleasure."

As we walked towards the register, I pulled my wallet out of my purse to pay. When he noticed the gesture, he shook his head no at me.

"Your money is no good here. The haircut is on the house."

"That's very sweet of you, but I insist."

"Hmm…" he said as he pondered an idea. "Tell you what. Bring me a piece of that tasty Key lime pie the next time you stop by. Then we can call it even."

"Sounds like a deal."

Before I stepped one foot out of the door, he waved me down. "Before you go, I wanted to tell ya to be careful out there. The rich and powerful of this town are as dangerous as any run-of-the-mill criminal. Maybe worse. I don't believe for one second that your daddy's death was an accident. Just make sure to watch your back."

When I walked outside, I noticed I had missed a text from Star.

Call me back when you can. We have a serious problem.

I rushed back to Grove Park as quick as my legs would take me. After the craziness that occurred days before, I didn't know what to expect. I feared the worst.

"What's the problem?" I shouted as I rushed into the truck.

"I have good news and bad news, I'm afraid," Star replied as she pulled out a chair for me to sit in.

"Give me the bad news first."

"Our only oven is now broken as well."

"Are you kidding me?" I said as I started to hyper-ventilate. "What are we going to do without an oven?"

"Don't worry," Star said as she tried to calm me down. "There's good news as well. Mrs. Conway from Sunny Shores Baptist Church wants you to fix an order of ten Key lime pies. Ty ran the numbers, and it would be enough to fix both ovens."

I regained my composure. "It's not so bad. We can do it. Maybe this is a blessing in disguise?"

"True," Star replied. "Not to mention you have a hot date tonight."

With everything going on, I forgot about the date that night. So much for my calm nerves.

[15]

I felt a sudden rush of nerves seeing my reflection in the mirror. At first I didn't recognize the woman who stared back at me. The image in front of me showed a woman with her hair primped, makeup on, and wearing a cute black dress. It was a far cry from my usual outfit consisting of a pink t-shirt one size too big, worn out apron, faded capris, and flip-flops. On second thought, I decided to wear the flip-flops anyway. No high heels for me, especially since I planned to walk to the restaurant.

When it came to dating, I was like a fish out of water. Even more appropriately, I was like a fish out of water flopping around on the surface of the moon. I was that clueless and out of touch. Dating seemed less complicated in high school. Now dating consisted of Tinder, Bumble, ghosting, hookups,

FWBs, slow fading, and too many rules and terms to keep up with.

My arrangement wasn't a real date, right? What did I have to worry about? I attempted to keep myself in the right frame of mind. Too bad Star made matters worse.

She called me up that evening. Star appeared to be vicariously living through me. I found her sudden increase in interest odd, especially when she had the more interesting life.

"Tonight's the night," she said. "Feeling nervous?"

"Nervous? Me?" I said as I laughed. "It's not a date, so I have nothing to be nervous about."

I lied. My nerves were wrecked and getting the best of me. What do I say? Do I eat in front of him? What if there are awkward silences? These were all questions and concerns that pulsated through my brain.

"Look at it this way, Kara. In my experience, two outcomes are possible," she explained. "If things go well, you will have a great time. If you're lucky, the night could end with a kiss."

"What's the other outcome?" I almost hesitated to ask.

"The night becomes a disaster of epic proportions he and his friends laugh about for years to come. Or, you embarrass yourself to the point your only option is to move far away. Possibly become a nun."

"Thanks a lot. I feel a lot better now," I said sarcastically.

Star picked up on the fact that I wasn't amused. "The worst thing that could happen is that you two don't click. Not everyone is compatible. The only way to find out is to try. Believe me, I know. I'm almost out of tries around here."

"Besides, it's not a date," I insisted. "I'm only going to try to get a word with Chris. He hasn't returned my calls, so I'm going to confront him face-to-face. He's been curious absent from the park, since the accident."

"His absence isn't too curious if you think about it," Star said. "His food truck did explode and all."

"Regardless, I'll get a chance to talk to him. That date is just the cover."

"Whatever you say, Kara. At least you get a free meal out of the process," she added, then paused to think about what she said. "Bring your purse, just in case he's too cheap to pay."

Her words made sense and hit a little too close to home. When it came to cheapskates, my ex-boyfriend fit the bill. Actually, when it came to the bill, he slid it my way on more than one occasion.

Dustin's family was well-off, so he never held a real job in his life. His parents paid for his college, books, apartment, and anything his heart desired. Although he received a monthly stipend to live on, he blew it in the first week of every month. Instead of swallowing his pride and begging for additional money, he turned to me for help.

My parents made a decent living, but couldn't pay for everything. Thankfully, through hard work and dedication, I earned a full scholarship from under-graduate school through law school. I worked a part-time job to help my parents with my apartment and living expenses. Dustin took full advantage of this.

"Hmm…" I said while I pondered Star's tip. "On second thought, I better take my wallet."

In a move I considered a stroke of genius, I arrived at Mama Mia's Little Italian twenty minutes before the time of my date. Rather, the time of my friendly dinner meeting. I hoped to get a chance to talk with Chris before Will arrived. Unfortunately for me, Will arrived earlier than me.

As I approached the entrance of the restaurant, Will stood waiting by the door. Tall, dark, and handsome was a tired cliché, but he wore it quite well. He spotted me and walked my way.

"Don't you look great?" Will said as greeted me with a hug. "I think this is the first time I've seen you without an apron, or even outside the window of your truck."

Half embarrassed and half flattered, I smiled. I attempted to not blush, although I was sure I appeared red as a strawberry. It didn't help that he looked hot in his tight dark jeans.

"You clean up pretty well yourself," I said as I tried to keep reminding myself it wasn't a date. His half smile, half grin made it difficult.

"Let's go inside, shall we," he said as he opened the front door for me. "I've already got us a table."

As the hostess led us to our table, I looked around the restaurant for Chris. The place was booming for a weeknight, with most tables occupied with a mix of locals and tourists. With so many people moving around, finding Chris in the crowd proved difficult at best.

"Excuse you," a woman in a red hat shouted as I bumped into the back of her chair. I lacked coordination as it was, so trying to locate someone in a crowd while walking proved a bad idea.

"I'm so sorry," I said as I tried to apologize.

"Hmmph," she said under her breath as she avoided looking me in the eyes. The woman looked familiar, but I couldn't quite put my finger on how I recognized her. On the other hand, if she recognized me, she seemed to have no desire to reconnect.

After that mishap, I decided to focus on walking the rest of the way to our table. We were sat at a quiet table in the back of the restaurant. Lucky for me, one side of the table faced the kitchen. I obviously chose the chair with that view, so I might catch a glance of Chris working in the kitchen.

As we sat down, the hostess handed us our menus.

"So what's good here," Will asked as he pulled my menu down. I guess I couldn't hide behind my menu all night.

"I love the chicken parm here. That, or the lasagna," I

said as I glanced back at the menu. "Honestly, everything I've tried here has been delicious."

John Harmon's reputation as a person might have been suspect. However, the man knew how to run an excellent restaurant. The food at his downtown location was excellent. My stomach growled in anticipation from the aroma that filled the air.

"Chicken parm it is," he said. "You know, it's kind of funny."

I looked at him, curious. "What's that?" I asked.

"My parents always talked about opening an Italian restaurant of their own." He smiled.

"What's so funny about that?"

"They both were awful cooks," he said, laughing. "If I hadn't learned to cook, I might have starved to death."

I smiled at him as I picked up the wine menu. "They have an amazing Pinot Noir that complements the dish. I can never remember the name. I believe they carry it by the bottle if you want to try it."

"None for me, thanks," Will said as he shook his head. "I'm not much of a wine person. Feel free to order it for yourself."

"You don't have to twist my arm," I replied. It was a rare occasion that I went out, so I wanted to take full advantage of it. Besides, a little alcohol wouldn't hurt. I needed something to calm my nerves.

After the waitress stopped by to take our order, I noticed Chris Kelly out of the corner of my eye. Chris and another waitress stood around the drink station talking to each other. At this point, I tuned out Will and had no idea what he was saying. The only thing I could think about was how I needed to speak to Chris. My window of opportunity closed by the second.

"Can you excuse me for a second?" I asked Will, interrupting his rambling.

He appeared to be slightly taken aback, but grinned regardless. "Sure. I need to step out and make a phone call. I haven't heard from my partner, Tom, all day."

I excused myself and walked in Chris's direction. I wasn't sure if it was intentional or not, but he began to walk in the opposite direction. I began to get the hunch that he was avoiding me. I finally cornered him in the banquet room in the back of the restaurant.

"Hey Chris, do you have a second?" I asked as I waved him down.

"Hey Kara, what are you doing here?"

"I'm having dinner with a friend. Your father's restaurant is one of my favorites in town."

"Step-father," he quickly interjected.

"I'm sorry to hear about your loss. I'm sure it's been hard on you and your mother."

"You could say that," he said. I didn't get the feeling he was too upset, to be honest. He appeared to be more annoyed by me asking.

"I'm not sure if you heard or not, but the video footage from my camera showed someone else around your truck that morning."

Chris began to nervously fiddle with the clipboard he held in his hand. "I did hear something to that effect. What are you trying to accomplish?"

"I believe the person on camera murdered your step-father. The identity of that person is still in the air. Do you have any theories on who it might be? Did anyone else in town have issues with John?"

"You're better off compiling a list of people who didn't have issues with him. That's a shorter list."

"So no one in particular stands out?"

"Look Kara, I would love to talk more, but I'm extremely busy at the moment. We're down a server. Not to mention, the health inspector is dining at table twelve," he explained as he pointed to the same woman in the red hat from earlier. The same woman I bumped into.

"That's Ms. Pettyjohn?" I asked as I put two and two together. "I hardly recognized her."

"That's her all right," he said as he smiled. "The same Margaret Pettyjohn whose house you rolled in the 12th grade."

"In my defense, I was only tagging along with Dustin and a few of his friends. It wasn't my idea," I responded.

"Maybe so, but you're the only one she identified," he added. "She caught you red-handed."

He wasn't lying. Out of the five of us, Ms. Pettyjohn spotted me as the others ran further ahead. She called my parents before I stepped one foot into my driveway. They grounded me for two weeks.

Ms. Pettyjohn held a grudge against me that lasted throughout high school. I apologized and even mowed her yard that summer. Nothing I did made a difference, and judging by her stare when I bumped into her that evening, she held that grudge to this day.

"I learned a valuable lesson that day."

"Don't roll the house of the grumpiest old lady in town?"

"Not exactly," I said as I grinned. "Don't go rolling someone's house with a group of track team members, especially when you're as slow as me."

When I returned to the table, Will asked, "Who were you talking to?"

I took a sip of wine and responded. "Chris Kelly. You know, John Harmon's step-son."

"I thought he looked familiar. How's he doing?"

"Surprisingly, he seemed well. Although, he and his step-father didn't get along."

"Do you think he did it? Do you think he killed John Harmon?"

I thought for a second before responding. I didn't

want to seem too eager to talk about the murder. Although, my curiosity got the best of me.

"I don't think he did it. In fact, I have another theory."

Before I could finish, the waitress delivered our entrees. The aroma of the food sidetracked my mind. "Let's talk about something else. Where are you from?"

Will smiled. "I grew up around Marathon, Florida."

"Any siblings?" I asked.

"Nope. I'm an only child."

I continued to ask question after question. My lack of dating experience was turning our date into more of an interview than a date. Luckily for me, Will was a good sport.

"Am I under trial?"

"No, of course not," I responded as I felt embarrassed. "I guess I get it, honestly, from my father."

"I've heard you've been quite the little sleuth around town. I guess you aren't used to being the one interrogated."

The conversation continued as the night went on.

However, it became two sided instead of one. At the end of the meal, the waitress presented Will and me with a dessert menu.

"Their Key lime pie is really good. Want to share a slice?"

Will shook his head in disagreement. "None for me. I'll have to pass."

"Seriously? Are you allergic to limes?

"No. I just don't like the taste."

Since Key lime pie was one of my favorite desserts, I was taken aback by his answer. How could someone who lived in Florida not like it?

"I don't know if I can trust a fellow Floridian that doesn't like Key lime pie."

"Trust me. I'm as much of a Floridian as anyone." He laughed. "I was born and raised in Marathon, Florida. Being so close to Key West, I ate enough Key lime pie to last two lifetimes."

"So what's the problem?" I asked. "Trying to keep your girlish figure?"

"The summer after my high school graduation, I lost both my parents in a car accident."

"Oh no," I said as my heart sank. "Will. I'm so sorry. Do you mind if I ask what happened?"

I placed my hand on top of his. Will hesitated for a moment, and then took a deep breath before responding. "It was a drunk driver that took my parents' lives that night."

I realized that that was the reason that Will didn't drink, and I could certainly understand why. The pain of losing your parents to a careless drunk on the highway was enough reason to cause anyone to swear off alcohol.

He continued. "Because of one selfish idiot, I lost both my mom and dad that night. My life changed forever because one man couldn't control his inner demons."

"I lost my dad last year, but I can't imagine the pain of losing both parents at such a young age. It must have been so tough for you."

I could feel the tension tightening in the air. Will's emotions went from sadness to anger, revealing a pent up aggression he'd kept bottled up inside for years. I could feel his pulse racing fast, as I held his hand tighter.

A feeling of guilt crept into my conscience as I

glanced over at my half-full glass of Chardonnay. I was embarrassed. The only dessert I'd deserved that night was a heaping slice of humble pie.

I understood his reaction, but didn't know how to respond. So as usual, I blurted out the first thing that came to mind.

"So pecan pie instead?"

Will laughed out loud and said, "Pecan pie sounds wonderful."

I breathed a sigh of relief as the look of rage was gone and his normal color returned to his face.

"It's not all bad, though. My parents are gone, but I carry the good memories inside. From my mom's apple pie to fishing on our boat, The Salty Mutt, with my dad, the memories live on."

Will opened the door for me as we walked out of the restaurant.

"Where are you parked?" Will asked. "I'll walk you to your car."

"That's sweet, but I didn't drive."

"You walked here?"

"I only live a mile from downtown."

"I can respect that," he said as he looked at me like he was impressed. "I'm sure it's a good way to stay health conscious and in shape."

"It is," I responded. "Plus, I don't own a car. So there's that too."

Will smiled. "Can I walk you home instead?"

"That's sweet, but you don't have to do that."

"I must insist. This town has not been the safest place for the past few weeks. I couldn't let a beautiful woman such as yourself walk home alone at this time of night," Will said, then quickly backtracked. "I'm not saying you can't take care of yourself. It's such a nice night out, and the pleasure would be all mine."

It was a lovely offer. There was no way I could say no after that. It had been a long time since a man had said I was beautiful. My ex would say it at times, but it almost felt forced.

"This is it," I said as we approached my home.

"I pass by here sometimes when I'm out running. It's a beautiful house."

"Thanks, it's my mother's house. I'm staying with her right now to save money."

"She's not going to come out and scold me for having you out past your curfew, is she?"

"Probably, but you're lucky she's out of town right now."

"I had a great time. We should do it again soon," he said as he pulled closer. "Good night."

As he leaned in, I closed my eyes. In my adult life, I'd only kissed one man. Because of this, I gained most of my romantic knowledge and expertise from Lifetime movies. I knew exactly what was coming next

Wrong.

To my surprise, his head moved in the opposite direction of mine. It dawned on me that he was going in for a hug and not a kiss. Luckily for me, I un-puckered my lips before he noticed.

"I'll call you," he said as he turned away.

As he walked down my front steps, I stood dazed and confused. I kept telling myself it wasn't a date, but to say I wasn't disappointed was a lie.

16

"I need details," Star said as she entered the food truck the next morning. She didn't take one step in before she was asking about my date from the night before. I would have at least worked my way up to asking the question, but Star was not one for small talk.

"Details about what?" I asked, pretending to play dumb. "Today's specials?"

"Don't make me grab the rolling pin from over there," Star replied. "You know what I'm talking about. How did last night go?"

I couldn't tell by her tone if she was kidding or being serious.

"What happened last night?" Ty asked as he

appeared through the door with perfect timing as usual.

"Kara's hot date with Will."

"Oh, that guy," Ty responded. Ty lacked the enthusiasm and interest that Star was showing. He walked to the other side of the truck and started unpacking the supplies he brought in, pretending to butt out.

"If you must know... I said hesitantly. "It was a nice evening. We had a nice dinner with great conversation."

"And then...?"

"The weather was perfect last night, so he offered to walk me home. We had a lovely stroll and then said our goodbyes."

"And then...?"

"He gave me a hug and we said goodnight."

"A hug?" Star shouted as her voice raised an octave higher.

I didn't understand what the big deal was. A hug was a sweet gesture, or so I thought. What was she expecting?

Judging by the snicker echoing from the back of the

truck, Ty found our conversation amusing. Both Star and I stared back at Ty with a not-so-amused look in return. He cleared his throat and straightened up.

"Uh… we're getting low on sugar," Ty replied, trying to save face. "I think I'll run down to the Piggly Wiggly and grab a few bags."

"I think that's an excellent idea, Ty," Star responded. As Ty walked out the door, she continued, "Now where were we?"

"I'll prove it," I said as picked my cell phone up off the counter. "I'll send him a text and tell him how I enjoyed last night."

Before I could swipe one finger on my phone, Star grabbed it out of my hands and threw it on the grass outside the main window.

"Again?" I screamed.

"Sorry, it's a force of habit." Star smiled and shrugged her shoulders. "I did it for your own good, Kara. Don't you know anything about rules of dating nowadays?"

"Rules?" I asked. I was clueless.

I was destined to end up Sunny Shore's resident single crazy cat lady. Dating as an adult was a foreign concept for me. More accurately put, I was an idiot when it came to dating. And now to top that off, there were additional rules I'd have to learn? At this point, I should probably start collecting cats now for my inevitable future.

"First of all, do not contact him first. Let the guy make the first move. The stench of clinginess and desperation is a surefire way to run any decent guy off permanently."

"So I need to stay cool and act uninterested?"

"Are you trying to be single for the rest of your life?"

"You need to find the middle ground. Try to find the perfect balance between the two. If you do, it drives the guy crazy, but in a good way."

My text alert tone went off in the distance, so I went out of the truck to retrieve it.

"Are you happy now?" I said as I put the phone up to her face. "He sent the first text."

Hi Kara. Had a great time last night, hopefully we can do it again soon. I'm trying to hunt down Tom, so I won't be at the park today. TTYL

"Don't make me slap the phone out of your hand again."

"So there's a rule about when I can respond?"

"You're learning," she said as she sarcastically slow clapped. "You never respond right away to a text. If you do, it gives the appearance that you are desperately waiting by the phone for them to respond."

"But I am."

"Maybe so, but you don't want them to know that."

"So when can I respond?"

"You double your response time based on his," she explained. "For example, if it takes him two hours to respond to you, you respond back in four."

"Any more advice you'd like to share?" I asked Star.

She smiled. "You might want to invest in a phone case."

"Code 157," I mumbled under my breath as I grabbed a printout sitting next to the scanner. I'd printed out a list of police codes that I'd found online. I quickly scanned through them until I hit number 157.

"That's a murder."

"A murder at the Cozy Cove Inn? I'm not surprised to hear that," Star responded. "That place is sketchy and sleazy to begin with."

"Another murder in Sunny Shores? That makes two in one week. What if they're connected?" I replied. "We need to go check it out."

"Are you serious?"

"Yes, it might be connected to the Harmon case."

"Am I still on the clock if I go?" Star asked.

"Yes."

Driving up to the Cozy Cove Inn was like taking a trip back in time. The Cozy Cove Inn was a road side motel that was built in the 1960's. It was located ten miles north of Sunny Shores on State Highway 41. The inn was close to being at the half-way point between Parrot Bay and Sunny Shores.

The Cozy Cove Inn was your typical road-side motor inn. There was nothing fancy about it. The only amenities on the ground were a dirty ice machine, a vending machine that I was sure served snacks that had been discontinued for years, and a pool that was an unusual shade of green.

The motel itself consisted of a long, rectangular-shaped building with a main office attached to the front. The building was one floor with twenty-five units. The door to each room faced the parking lot that was directly in front.

Motels like the Cozy Cove Inn were popular in the mid-twentieth century. This was when the automobile craze took off. This was the first time that a majority of Americans could afford to own a car. With the ability to now drive themselves anywhere, people were able to travel longer distances for trips and vacations.

Florida, with its year-round warm weather and beaches, was a popular destination for many. During that time, thousands of these road-side motels popped up. With its proximity to Orlando, the Cozy Cove Inn was one of the more popular motels in northern Florida.

As with many things, people's tastes changed over the years. When developers began to build nicer hotels and resorts, the popularity of these road-side motels declined. By the 2000's, the majority of these motels had closed down for good.

Even though the Cozy Cove Inn had survived, it remained a shell of its former self. Instead of being booked by families traveling on vacation, it was mainly used for unethical local rendezvous. One could only imagine the number of divorces and illegitimate children that were produced between those paper-thin walls.

"To be honest, I'm not surprised at all," Star said as she wove through traffic while driving us in her bright yellow Volkswagen Beetle.

"Surprised about what?" I asked as I reached down to ensure my seat belt was buckled tightly.

"There being a murder at the Cozy Cove Inn. To be honest, the place was probably due for one. It looks like something out of a horror movie."

"You have a point. I wouldn't be caught dead staying there, myself."

"Too bad Missy Harmon can't say the same thing," Star replied.

I turned immediately towards my window, trying to keep from chuckling. Star had a quick yet dry wit to her that could be hilarious, although her timing was not always so impeccable.

"Too soon?

When we pulled into the parking lot of the Cozy Cove Inn, the place was relatively deserted. The first thing I noticed was the blue lights of a Sunny Shores police cruiser reflecting off the palm trees that were lined up in front of the inn. Beside the police car, Missy Harmon's bright white Mercedes Benz was parked in front of a room with police caution tape strung up around the door.

The stench of cigarette smoke and regret filled the air as we got out of the car and walked to the door. Deputy Mark Johnson and the inn's owner, Sonny Pines, were standing outside the motel room door. Both were waiting for the paramedics and Chief Martin to arrive. Deputy Johnson was new to the force, and didn't recognize Star and I as we approached the motel room.

"Ladies, please stand back. You're approaching a murder investigation scene," Deputy Johnson said, raising his hand in the air like a traffic cop.

Deputy Johnson was closely guarding the motel room door, so I couldn't get a good look inside. Each time I tried to shift my head around the deputy to get a look, he would quickly adjust his body to attempt to block my wandering eyes.

"Oh my goodness gracious," Star said in a voice that I had never heard spew from her lips. "What in the world happened there, officer?"

Star sounded like a helpless, Southern debutante. It was if she'd summoned the ghost of Scarlett O'Hara from Gone with the Wind. My first impression was that she sounded ridiculous, but Deputy Johnson ate it up.

"Well ma'am," Deputy Johnson began to speak as he took off his hat like a proper Southern gentleman. "There's been an accident. The lady inside is dead."

"Accident?" Sonny Pines blurted out. "It was no accident. That pretty lady killed herself and left that note that you have in your hands."

In Deputy Johnson's left hand, he was holding a large plastic evidence bag. Inside the bag was a handwritten letter.

"Oh my, oh my," Star exclaimed. "That's Missy Harmon's car. It's her, isn't it?"

"I can't confirm that at this time. We have to finish the investigation first before any information can be made public," Deputy Johnson replied.

"It's her," Sonny said nonchalantly. "Or at least, that was the name she used when she checked in."

Suddenly, the sound of a police siren and screeching tires echoed through the parking lot. Chief Martin had arrived. He wasted no time in getting out of the car. As he approached us, he had a stern look of frustration that caused his mustache to curl upwards.

"Johnson, what the hell is going on here?"

"Chief, I was just telling these young ladies to move along."

As Chief Martin turned to Sonny Pines and Deputy Johnson to explain the merits of keeping the crime scene confidential, I began to whisper quietly to Star.

"We have to get a picture of that suicide letter he's holding. You keep sweet-talking the deputy and snap a picture with your phone. I'll keep Sam Martin busy."

"Kara, why are you here?" Chief Martin asked as he turned his attention at me. "You and Star are a long way from Grove Park."

"We were driving to Parrot Bay to look at a new oven for my truck. On the way, we noticed the police lights and Mrs. Harmon's car parked out front of the Cozy Cove. I was concerned something was wrong with Missy, so I stopped to see what was going on."

"I had no idea that you were close to Mrs. Harmon."

"Oh, I wasn't close at all to her. Until the other day, she'd never spoken a word to me. After the passing of her husband, she contacted me about catering an event for her."

As Chief Martin continued to scold me, I peeked out of the corner of my eye to spy on Star and Deputy Johnson, who had slipped off in the distance.

"I feel so much better knowing that there are strong officers like you protecting Sunny Shores," Star said as she placed her hand on his upper arm.

Johnson turned eight shades of red. "I'm just doing my job, ma'am. It's nothing, really."

"You can call me Star," she said as she moved in closer to him. "Maybe we can have dinner sometime, and I'm sure you can tell me a few exciting stories about your job."

"Really?" Deputy Johnson squealed out in a voice that was three octaves higher than normal. He then cleared his throat and responded in a much deeper and macho tone. "I'll check my calendar. I'm sure we could arrange something."

"Can I get a picture of you?" Star asked.

"A picture? What for?"

"I need a picture of you to put in my phone, so I know it's you when you call."

Johnson looked behind him to ensure the Chief was occupied and said, "Well… when you put it that way, sure, why not?"

Star pulled out her phone and pointed the camera at Deputy Johnson. "Hold up that bag in your hand and smile big. There's nothing sexier than a man in action on the job."

As soon as I noticed Star was finished taking the picture, I nodded my head as a signal for it being time to leave. We didn't need to overstay our welcome.

"We're sorry for intruding. We'll leave and get out of your way," I said as I motioned for Star. "Star, let's go."

As Star opened the driver's side door, she waved to Deputy Johnson and said, "Call me."

Deputy Johnson grinned, but quickly did a double-take.

"Wait... you never gave me your number."

Star smiled as she sat down and shut the door behind her, blowing a kiss at him as we drove off.

"That was so exciting," I said to Star as we made our way down the highway. "I've never done anything like that before. It felt dangerous."

"I have to admit, Kara, that was pretty exhilarating."

"You actually took a picture with Deputy Johnson and the letter?" I asked as I examined the picture on Star's phone. "Why didn't you just zoom in on the letter itself? He never would have known."

"I don't know," Star responded, shrugging her shoulders. "I think he's kind of cute."

"Oh my."

"What does it say?"

"I don't believe it. It's a confession."

"A confession for what?"

"The murder of her husband."

~

Although I needed a drink, I settled for the next best thing… caffeine.

"Something seems off about this entire situation," I said as I continued to stare at the photo on Star's phone.

"Stop trying to over-analyze everything. There's nothing left for you to prove. You were right the entire time," said Star.

"She's right, Kara. You were the first to realize it wasn't an accident, and you suspected Missy Harmon from the beginning. The letter she wrote proves that you were right," Ty said, trying to be the voice of reason. "You solved the case."

"If her motivation for killing her husband was money, why would she kill herself before she cashed in on a fortune?" I asked. "That's the part that doesn't make sense."

"Who knows what was going through that bimbo's head at the time. She was probably starting to feel guilty for what she did to her husband. Or, more likely, she knew that you were close to exposing her for what she did. Either way, it's over now."

I continued to stare at the phone as I took a deep breath. My mind tumbled around and around like a washing machine as I tried to piece everything together. My head was overwhelmed with clues, suspects, motives, and the like. Much to the dismay of my friends, I couldn't let it go.

Bonnie May walked over to our table with a fresh pot of coffee. Although her intentions were to top off our cups, I was sure a small part of her was curious about our conversation.

"I take it y'all have heard about what happened to Missy Harmon," she said as she approached the table. "I never would have pegged her as the type of person to take her own life."

Although Star and I were present at the crime scene, neither one of us was able to get a clear view of the body. The only clue we were able to see was the suicide letter. There was no sign of how she did it. I then realized who we were talking to. If anyone had inside info, it would be Bonnie May.

"We were all shocked as well," I said. "Do you have any idea what happened?"

"A little birdie told me that she wrote a letter confessing that she killed her husband. Her body was found by Mr. Pines after he received an anonymous call. They found an empty bottle of Vicodin behind the headboard of the bed. It appears that she OD'ed."

"On the bright side, I don't have to read those condescending comments she wrote on her receipts anymore."

When she mentioned Missy's notes, a photo flashed into my mind of the receipt that Bonnie May had shared with me the other day. That was one of the strange things about my photographic memory. I never knew what would trigger it. Just a thought, a mention, or overhearing a subject or idea could bring a memory out of my mind.

"That's it," I shouted. I turned to Bonnie May and asked, "Can you pull out your receipts from the other day?"

"I can, but why?"

"I need to see the one for Missy Harmon."

Seeing the determined look on my face, Bonnie May agreed to my request. She went behind the counter and pulled out a tin lockbox. She flipped through the pile of receipts until she found the one from Missy. She walked over and handed it to me.

"I knew it," I said. "The signature on the suicide note doesn't match the one on the receipt."

I zoomed the image on the phone to show a close up of Missy's signature and showed it to the group.

"How in the world did you get a picture of letter?"

"You're not the only one in this town with connections, Bonnie May."

Ty wasn't as convinced as I was. "I don't know, Kara. The signatures look similar enough. If she was suicidal and stressed, I'm sure it would have been reflected in her handwriting. I wouldn't expect it to be exactly the same as when she was having coffee."

Ty had a valid point, but I wasn't convinced. There was one feature in particular about her signature that immediately tipped me off. It was the first thing that flashed into my mind when I recalled the image of her receipt. Missy had a peculiar way of writing the "y" in her first name.

It's the 'y' in Missy," I said as I pointed to the signature on the receipt. "Look at the strange way she curls the tail. It looks like an infinity sign."

"You're right. I never noticed it before. I guess I was so fixated on the stupid comments she wrote."

"If you look at the signature on the note, the curl is different."

Ty looked closer at the receipt. "You're right."

If Missy Harmon wasn't the killer, the only question now was... who was it?

17

That evening at home, my mind felt exhausted. The only thing I wanted to do was sleep. So I decided to turn in and go to bed early.

To be honest, staying at home alone had me spooked. Luckily for me, I was too tired to think about it that night. It had been a long and exhausting day.

As I slipped into bed, a loud crashing sound came from downstairs. I froze at first, not knowing what to do. It didn't take long to convince myself I was hearing things. I felt convinced my mind played a trick on me, but I needed proof before I could sleep.

In what was likely a poor mark of judgment, I

decided to walk downstairs and see what was going on.

I tiptoed slowly down each stair, my heart racing quicker with each step. What the heck was I doing? Maybe curling up under the covers was a better option than marching towards my inevitable death.

When I walked into the living room, I flipped the light switch. When the room lit up, I scanned around, trying to find the source of the loud sound. It wasn't long before I found the issue.

Over by the sofa, glass shards were scattered out across the floor. The window in the living room was broken, with a large rock being the culprit. Not only that, but a note was attached to the rock.

I walked over to examine it closer. I detached the note from the rock and read it out loud to myself.

If you don't want to end up like Missy or John... BACK OFF.

I screamed out loud as I dropped the rock on the floor. For the first time in my life, I felt in true danger. I honestly felt scared for my life.

I ran upstairs to retrieve my phone. The first person I called was Sam Martin. He told me to stay in my room and lock my door. He would be out there immediately.

Before I could return to my room, I heard a knock on the front door. What now? I thought.

I looked out the peep hole, not knowing what to expect. Thankfully, the person standing at the door was a welcome sight. I felt at ease as I opened the door.

"Is everything OK in here?" Will asked. "I heard a loud scream while I was out for my evening jog."

A few minutes later, Sam and a couple police officers showed up. After looking around the house, they determined that the person responsible had left the scene. Sam told me he'd have officers ride by every hour or so, to make sure I was safe.

"You shouldn't stay here alone tonight," Sam said as he paced around. "I have a bad feeling."

"I can stay, officer," Will replied. "I don't mind at all."

"This is very sweet of you, but you don't have to stay," I said. Deep down I knew I wanted him to stay. The last thing I wanted to do was seem needy or overzealous.

"It is not a question of feeling obligated, Kara," he

said as he flashed that amazing smile of his. "I want to stay."

I was trying not to blush, but I was sure my face was as red as velvet cake. I pressed my body against his and he wrapped his strong arms around me. For the first time all night, a feeling of safety and security flushed through my body.

I removed my head from his chest and whispered into his ear, "Thank you so much, but I do have one favor to ask."

"Sure, Kara. Just name it," he said.

"Please take those muddy tennis shoes off before they ruin my carpet."

He chuckled and said, "Whoops."

"Let me run upstairs and get you a blanket and pillow."

News traveled fast around Sunny Shores. The next morning, I was bombarded with questions from both Star and Ty.

"I wish you would've called me, Kara," Ty said. I

could tell that he was worried about me. To be honest, it was very sweet.

"Your mom is putting in a security system?"

"Oh heck no, we can't afford that."

"What could you afford?"

I reached behind the counter and pulled out an aluminum baseball bat that I'd purchased at Jimmy's Sporting Goods. It seemed like a good compromise. The bat was light, but still could pack a wallop. Plus, it would come in handy if I ever joined a softball team. Plus, it was bright pink.

"After last night, I'm not taking any chances."

Ty grabbed the bat out of my hand. He gripped the handle and stood there posing like he was a player at bat. "This brings back memories. I wonder if I still have it. It's been years since I've played."

I laughed. "Ty, you never did have it. My dad always said you swung like a girl."

Star shook her head. "I can see that."

"You're both crazy. I had a mean swing back in the day."

"You keep telling yourself that, slugger," I said as I

stole the bat out of Ty's hands. "You forget that I went to all of your games and witnessed that mean swing of yours first-hand. Too bad the object of the game was to actually hit the ball."

❦

18

"Oh, crap!" Star said. "Trouble's coming right this way at twelve o'clock."

"I guess we're good then," I replied, as I continued mixing. "It's half-past 1:30 now."

I was so deep in thought while I spun the spoon around the ceramic bowl that I wasn't paying close attention to what she was saying. I had a tendency to have tunnel vision when I had a lot on my mind. This time was no exception. All I could concentrate on was the mystery surrounding the two murders.

"No, dummy," she said as she snapped her fingers to get my undivided attention. "Twelve-o'clock, as in right in front of us."

Star pointed out the side window towards the grassy lawn in front of us. Walking swiftly toward my truck was Carlos Martinez. His face was void of emotion, as if he was in deep thought.

"He doesn't have a knife in his hand, does he," I whispered to Star, only half-kidding.

"I don't think so," Star replied. "Maybe I should grab your bat, just in case."

"Hola, Star," Carlos said as he leaned against the window. "Do you mind if I talk to Kara in private for a moment? Por favor."

Star turned around and stared at me with her eyes wide open. I could tell that she was concerned, and she didn't want to answer unless I gave her a sign. Her emerald green eyes were piercing, as if she was trying to talk through them.

"Sure, Carlos," I said as I nervously smiled. "Star, can you give us a minute?"

"I'll hang around close by," Star said as she made her way in the direction of the back door. The entire time her eyes were locked in on Carlos.

"It'll be OK, Star. I don't see that vein poppin' out of Carlos's neck today."

"I guess I deserve that," Carlos said as he took a deep breath. "Especially after the way I acted the other day."

"I'll admit, I was a little nervous. I've never seen you act that way."

I had never seen that side of Carlos, so it wasn't far-fetched that I'd be anxious around him. He would appear slightly intense at times, but showed nothing but respect for me and the other owners. It was hard to admit to myself, but his brash actions only height-ened my suspicions of him.

Carlos appeared nervous as he tapped his fingers against the counter.

"I need to be honest with you, Kara. You were right about me."

"What?"

My heart began to race. My stomach dropped to the floor of the truck. Was he confessing to the murder? Was I next?

"Not about me being the murderer," he said as he began to chuckle. "You were right about me being a former convict."

I breathed a much-needed sigh of relief.

"When I was in my thirties, I worked for a large investment firm in Boston. I had worked my way from being an entry-level sales associate to being the assistant to the regional manager."

"Really? I never would have guessed." His mannerisms and appearance never struck me as him being the corporate, nine-to-five type.

"You should know better than anyone that you can't judge a book by its cover."

He was right about that.

"My boss and a few of his associates were engaged in illegal activities, such as insider trading and outright fraud. When my boss became aware of undercover investigations going on in our firm, he needed an escape plan. Unfortunately for me, I was the scapegoat."

"How did they pin it on you?" I asked.

"My boss had forged hundreds of illegal documents with my name on them. He had also set up two offshore accounts in my name and funneled money into them. I had no idea. At least I didn't until the FBI stormed into my home to arrest me."

Carlos's mood turned somber. His eyes began to water as he tried to hold back the tears. I pulled out a tissue from behind the counter and handed it to him.

"Thanks, Kara," he said as he rubbed the tissue against his eyes. "I lost three good years of my life because of them. Three years in prison where I was away from my friends and family."

"That's awful, Carlos," I said as I began to feel sad as well. "Is that why you moved here? To get away from it?"

"As I rotted away in that awful prison, I made two important promises to myself. For one, I would never work in the corporate world again. I would never succumb to that corruption and greed."

"What was the other?"

"That I would never take family and friends for granted. That's why I moved here. I wanted a second chance at life. This was a new opportunity for me."

No wonder Carlos was so upset. The last thing he wanted was for his secret to get out. Carlos had strived for a second chance at life, without being judged for mistakes from his past.

A loud thud interrupted our conversation. Star's face came into view from behind the back door of the truck. Her face was bright red like a tomato as she reached her hand through the door to pick up the object she'd dropped. It was my baseball bat.

Later in the day, my long-time friend Kyle Harris stopped by. I never noticed him walk as fast as he walked through the parking lot toward us. He apparently had something important on his mind.

"Kara," he said as he tried to catch his breath. "You won't believe it."

"What?" I asked as I set my broom down against the wall. I walked out of the truck to talk to him face-to-face.

"Where are your manners, Kara?" said Star as she followed me out of the truck. She scooted herself in between Kyle and me. "Aren't you going to introduce me to your cute friend?"

Star greeted him by taking his hand and shaking it. Kyle's face turned red as a beet.

"Are you blushing?"

Kyle responded instantly, trying to save face. "Umm... it's just the heat, or my allergies acting up again."

Neither of us were convinced.

"You said you had big news?" I asked.

"I discovered who the primary beneficiary to John Harmon's estate is."

Star and I both shouted, "Who?"

"Another family member."

"Why would Chris be the beneficiary?" asked Star.

"He's not," I replied. "Kyle isn't referring to Chris. Are you?"

"Nope," Kyle replied.

It only took a split second for me to realize what Kyle was implying. He wasn't referring to Chris, John's step-son.

"I give up. I'm confused," Star said, as she threw her hands up in the air.

"Are you trying to say that John Harmon left his money to another blood relative?" I asked as I tried to process the surprising news.

Kyle shook his head yes. "That's correct."

But who?

The City Hall building sat atop a hill east of downtown Sunny Shores. Because it was so rich with history, the town took pride in the building. A large number of tourists visited each year, as the building boasted one of Florida's oldest lighthouses.

According to town history, a Spanish watchtower originally occupied the site in the 1700's. The watch tower was used by the Spanish to assist in navigating the North American coast. According to historians, the Seminole Indians attacked the Spanish and destroyed the tower, leaving a pile of rocks and bones, still displayed to this day.

The current structure, built in 1809, housed the town's first and only official light house. The light house operated until it a hurricane damaged it in 1947. Grieving from the loss of her husband in the storm, the widow of the owner decided to not spend any additional time or money fixing it. The lighthouse sat abandoned and neglected for the decades that followed.

In 1990, the city purchased the lighthouse and surrounding acreage with a grant from Congress. The city hall was built in a style complementary to the original structure, with the restored lighthouse as the main showpiece. The building was beautiful, but had taken on an ominous reputation as well.

"This place gives me the creeps," Ty said as he parked his car at the entrance. Ty was pulling in at a snail's pace.

I laughed. "You don't seriously believe the building's haunted, do you?"

"Not just the building, but the land it sits on as well," he said. "The hill we're sitting on now is cursed."

"Cursed? Really?" I said, shaking my head in disbelief.

"There's been nothing but death and destruction on this land." Ty said all this in a serious tone, not kidding around. "There's a gargoyle statue on the roof, for crying out loud."

"Big deal," I said as he continued to motion up at the statue. "That was a staple of architecture at the time."

"But in Florida of all places?" he said, unconvinced. "That's just weird."

When it came to ghost or horror stories, Ty was a chicken. To this day, he avoided going to see any type of scary movie. I'd tried hundreds of times over the years to convince him, but remained unsuccessful.

"Don't worry, you big baby, I won't make you go in with me," I said as I patted him on the shoulder. "I'm sure Star could use some help with me being gone. Would you mind going back and helping?"

I did sort of leave Star high and dry back at the truck. I pictured her in my mind, cursing my name under her breath. Lucky for her, dark clouds covered the sky. Tourists tended to shy away on cloudy days.

"Not at all," he said as he smiled. "What time should I come back and get you?"

"No need. I'll walk back or catch a ride when I'm finished. There's no need for you to come back."

"Thanks again for the ride," I said as I opened the

truck door and stepped out. Before I closed the door behind me, I poked my head back into car. "One more thing, Ty…"

"What's that?" he asked.

I grinned. "Boo!"

As I walked up the steps, I paused for a moment. The combination of being alone, the dark sky, and the creepy architecture spooked me as well.

The atrium of City Hall was noticeably slow and appeared empty. However, as I'd learned by living in a small town, you were destined to run into someone you knew.

"I didn't expect to see your smiling face today," Sam said as he wrapped his arm around me. "How are feeling? Have you had any other issues since the other night?"

It was obvious by the concerned look on his face that he was still worried for my safety. Break-ins rarely occurred in our small town, especially ones laced with malicious intent.

Was I freaked out staying home alone? Yes, of course.

However, my pride prevented me from admitting it. So naturally, I embellished the truth.

"Everything is good now. No worries," I said, while trying to play it cool. "I have a shiny new aluminum bat now. Let them try anything."

Sam looked stern and not amused in the slightest. "A bat is a cute idea, but not as helpful as the police. I've had my officers patrol your street a few times each night. I've personally tried to keep an eye on your street as well. If they try anything again, we'll catch 'em this time."

"I appreciate it, Sam. I really do."

"Now that you stopped playing detective, I think you'll be left alone."

"Yep," I said as I shifted my gaze to the floor. I avoided making eye contact with him, trying to not give my true intentions away.

Sam, not convinced by my response, never took his eyes off me. "Why are you at City Hall today?"

I couldn't think of a good excuse, so I tried to defer the question back to him.

"What are you doing here?"

"I had a meeting with the mayor."

"The mayor seems to have his nose up in your department's business a lot, doesn't he?"

"He's the town mayor, Kara. He has his nose in all facets of the city government, not just us."

"I don't know. It seems odd to have the town mayor so involved in the everyday business of the police. Don't you find it a bit suspicious?" I asked. "What's he up to?"

"You haven't answered my question," he said. "Why are you here?"

"To do my part as a citizen."

"You're lying," he said as he threw up his hands in frustration. "I knew it. Don't you realize it's my job to sniff out B.S.?"

"So what?" I replied, standing my ground. "I'm not breaking any laws. What's the harm?"

"You're going to get yourself hurt. Someone already tried once."

"I'm not going to back down because someone threatened me. That's what the old Kara would have done."

"The case is closed. I'm not sure what you're trying to accomplish here. Missy Harmon confessed to the murder of her husband. What more do you expect to find?"

"I've found evidence to the contrary. The signature on the suicide note isn't hers."

"How did you come up with that?"

Before I could answer, Sam's radio went off.

"Chief, do you have a copy? Over."

"Chief Martin here. Over."

"There's a new development in the missing person case you requested yesterday. Over."

"Copy that. I'm on my way to the station now. Over and out."

My ears perked up when I overheard the phrase missing person. My mind immediately thought of Will's co-worker, Tom Bryant. No one had seen or heard from him in days. He'd suspiciously left town when all the murders began to occur.

"Did that call have anything to do with Tom Bryant?" I asked.

"Always asking questions. Maybe you should be a detective?"

"Well, is it?"

He smiled. "Duty calls. Just promise me you'll stay out of trouble. OK?"

"I'll try," I replied.

I was being honest, really. It's not like I pursued trouble on my own. Trouble had a knack for finding me. I wasn't sure if that was a curse or a blessing, although lately it was the former.

After Sam left, I walked over to the records office. Martha Ham ran the records office at City Hall. She was a sweet, but peculiar woman. She wore dark glasses with thick lenses, and her hair and style of clothes were a bit on the homely side. It was obvious that she didn't get out much.

"Hello," I shouted as I opened the door.

Ms. Ham walked out from behind a large book case. She squinted her eyes and adjusted her glasses while examining me.

"Can I help you, young lady?" she asked softly as she approached.

"This may seem like an odd request, but I'm looking for information on John Harmon."

"Oh my," she responded as she sat down at her desk. "What a horrific accident."

"That's the thing," I replied. "I don't believe it was an accident. Someone murdered him."

"That's a shame, but what brings you here?"

"I believe he had another family member that was kept secret from everyone in town. I know it might be a long-shot, but maybe there's a clue here."

"You've come to the right place," she said as she stood up. "Everyone is so reliant on computers nowadays. Expect to push a few buttons and shazam, all the information magically appears. I still believe the best way to get information requires getting your hands dirty and searching for it yourself."

"Then what would you suggest? I'm open for anything at this point. Let's National Treasure this."

"Hmm…" she said as she scrunched her nose and began to think. It was apparent by her sudden spark of interest that she enjoyed this. This dusty corner of City Hall wasn't accustomed to this kind of excitement.

"I got it," she said as she rushed over to the other side of the room. Ms. Ham opened a closet door, revealing a room stacked with piles of file boxes. She frantically started unstacking boxes and moving them around. "The box is around here somewhere. I'm sure of it."

For being in charge of a record archive, Ms. Ham displayed horrible organization skills. At least on the surface, that is. While the room looked unorganized and cluttered, she employed an unorthodox system. Surprisingly enough, the system worked for her.

"Found it," she called out as she pulled a box out of the closet.

"What did you find?"

"Property tax records."

Property tax records?

"This box contains the records for property downtown. Look through this one, and I'll find the one for his home. He lives in Windmyer Estates, correct?"

"I believe so," I responded. At least, I thought he did. Most of the wealthier people of Sunny Shores lived in Windmyer Estates, so it seemed like a likely conclusion. Their residents preferred the gated community because it kept the riffraff like us out.

I looked through the box, sorting out form after form. Halfway through the box, one tax record in particular caught my eye. I pulled it out and stared at it.

"64 Ocean Ave."

The tax record I held in my hands belonged to Bonnie May Calloway. For a split second, I daydreamed about the possibility of owning that property myself. When Bonnie May retired, I want to open up a bakery where the Breezy Bean now sat. Wishful thinking, I knew.

I shook off the distraction and continued looking through the box until I found the tax record for John Harmon's restaurant. Unfortunately, nothing unusual stood out.

"Found it," Ms. Ham shouted as she lifted the form above her head. "5531 Thicket Meadow Court."

I examined the tax records and noticed the same address listed on the form for the Mama Mia Little Italian. "That's it. The tax form for the restaurant lists the same address under his name."

Ms. Ham took the thick glasses hanging from her

neck strap and placed them over her nose. She took a moment and examined the form.

"That's interesting," she said as she walked over and sat down beside me. "Look here. He has another previous address listed."

She passed the tax form over, so I could look. She was right. Under his name, it listed a previous address. He owned another home in the Sunny Shores. John Harmon lived in another home prior to moving into Windmyer.

Neither one of us needed to say anything because we both thought of the same idea.

Ms. Ham walked back over to the closet, retrieving another box. She set the box down between us, and we each took a stack of papers.

"Found it," I said as I discovered the form we searched for. It felt as if we were on a treasure hunt. "Bingo."

On that particular form, I finally found the clue we'd searched for this entire time.

John Green

778 San Juan Street

Duck Key, Florida 33050.

"What's next?" I asked Ms. Ham. "Do you have a special state database you can search?"

She laughed. "It's called Google."

We rushed over to her computer. When the search results populated, we scrolled down the page. At first, we found nothing. Frustration started to set in.

"I thought we were on to something."

"Patience, Kara. It's like I said earlier. You have to get your hands dirty and dig deep for the good information. It's not going to come to you."

Ms. Ham continued to scroll down each page, only to find nothing of substance. She didn't quit. With a stroke of the mouse, she continued to click to the next page.

Our patience paid off when we arrived at page 23.

"Stop," I screamed while pointing at the screen. "Right there, notice the name."

More than halfway down the page of search results, the name John Green caught my attention.

"Click on that link," I said.

The link took us to a news article dated June 14th, 2008.

Fatal Accident Shuts Down US HWY 1

One person dead and one injured as a two vehicle crash occurred on US HWY 1. The accident occurred at 11:30 p.m. Friday evening a mile north of Conch Key.

John Green was driving north-bound with his wife Marla Green in a white Lincoln Navigator. The accident occurred when the front bumper of a Ford F-150, driven by Hal Simpson, clipped the Navigator from behind.

Marla Green was pronounced dead on sight, while John Green and Hal Simpson sustained minor injuries.

The north-bound lane of US HWY 1 was closed for three hours while Florida State Patrol officers conducted their investigation.

"This has to be him," I said as I slapped the table in excitement. "John Harmon is John Green. John Green is John Harmon. It makes sense."

Ms. Ham sat confused. "How can you be sure?"

"Call it a gut feeling, or intuition. Whatever. I just know."

"I'll take your word for it," she said. She turned around and noticed the clock on the wall. "Shoot."

"What's wrong?"

"I hate to do this to you, Kara, but I need to lock up. It's after 5."

"Can you not stay open for a little longer? Please."

"I wish that I could, but I can't. The mayor banned all over-time for government employees, no exceptions," she explained. "You're more than welcome to come back tomorrow."

"I understand. Mayor Tightwad strikes again," I said. "I can't thank you enough, Ms. Ham."

"Don't mention it. Besides, I enjoyed this. You might not realize this, but my job's not as interesting as it looks."

As I walked out the front door of City Hall, the sky opened up as rain began to pour. If I was going to insist on walking and not driving, I would likely benefit from checking the weather beforehand. I was stranded with no other choice but to high-tail it out of there and run like hell.

Through torrential downpour, a pair of headlights shone through, like a beacon of hope. Laying on the horn to get my attention, Ty's truck appeared and pulled up to the front of the building. Perfect timing.

Before I could react, Ty rushed out of his car into the pouring rain. The heavy rain soaked him instantly, as he ran around the truck to open the door for me. He reached in the cab and pulled out an umbrella from behind his seat.

"What are you doing?" I shouted. Confused by his actions, I tried to get him to hear me over the sound of thunder rolling across the shores.

With a flick of his wrist, he opened the umbrella, allowing me to enter the cab without as much as one drop touching me. He closed the umbrella and threw it in the back of the truck.

When he sat back down, I looked at his rain drenched body. "You didn't have to do all that."

He wiped the water from his face, looked at me, and smiled. "You're right, I didn't have to.

[21]

That afternoon, I began the preparations for our catering order. After all the expenses I'd accrued, the extra money was truly needed. I sent Ty to the store to pick up the Key limes needed. Unfortunately, he missed one crucial detail.

"This is a regular lime," I said, frustrated. "You can't make Key lime pie without true Key limes."

"Smitty said that he was out of Key limes. These were the only ones he had in stock."

Smitty Evans ran the area's only organic farmer's market. His market provided the source of the majority of ingredients I used. I took pride in the fact we used all natural and organic ingredients in our dishes, so I couldn't back off from that now. Besides, I painted that pledge on the side of my truck. I was kind of stuck.

"What's the big deal? Ty said as he threw his hands in the air. "A lime is a lime, right?"

"Oh boy, I'm not getting involved in this one," Star said as she walked out of the truck. Star made the same mistake on her first day working for me. She wanted no part in listening to my speech once again.

"For starters, Key limes have a tarter flavor than a regular lime. The Key lime has a distinct aroma that can't be matched," I explained. "You just can't use a regular lime in its place. Are you crazy?"

"The regular limes are larger. I thought I was saving you money."

I saw the look of confusion mixed with regret on his face. He meant well.

I took a deep breath and smiled. "No worries. I'll call Smitty up and see if he can deliver a case before Monday."

Once a week, Smitty visited the park to deliver fresh fruits and vegetables. His service met an important need for the truck owners. We appreciated it.

"Hey Smitty, it's Kara Summers."

"Hi Kara. What can I do you for?"

"I'm out of Key limes. Can you bring a case by on Monday?"

"Oh…" he said, his voice deeper. "I'm not set to get another delivery until mid-week. Can you wait until then?"

"I have a catering order due on Tuesday for ten pies."

"Hmm…" he said as he paused for a minute to think. "I might have an idea."

"What's that?" I asked. At that point, I was desperate.

"It's quite a trip, but my supplier is located ten miles north of Marathon. I could call him and see if you can pick them up yourself. He's open on Sundays."

Disappointed by his suggestion, I sighed heavily. The city of Marathon sat four hours south of Sunny Shores. Even if I wanted to go, I didn't own a car. The only chance of making it down there hinged on convincing Star or Ty to take me. Good luck with that.

"Wait a second," I replied as a thought entered my head. Duck Key was located north of Marathon. John Harmon moved to Sunny Shores from Duck Key.

"Is your supplier located close to Duck Key?" I asked.

"Now that I think of it, he is."

"I'll do it then."

"Great. I'll reach out to him. I'll call you back with the address."

A trip to Duck Key, while out of the way, could provide additional clues to John Harmon's prior life. I knew his address. What harm could it do for me to ride by and check out his old place?

My lack of owning a vehicle prevented me from snooping further. If I was going to get there, I needed a ride. I could only think of two people that fit the bill.

Ty overheard part of my conversation and asked, "What's in Duck Key?"

I smiled. "Our Key limes."

"Isn't Duck Key a three hour drive from here?"

"It's four, actually," I responded.

In a rare case of my photographic memory actually being useful, I recalled the pamphlet for Comic Fest

Ty carried around the other day. I had the perfect idea.

"Isn't Comic Fest going on in Key Largo on Sunday?"

Ty reached into his back pocket and pulled out the pamphlet. "You're right. It's going on from 12 to 8 p.m. I'll take you on one condition."

"You name it."

"We have to stay at least three hours at Comic Fest."

"I was thinking one hour at the most."

"How about two hours and you pretend to enjoy it."

"You have a deal. No dressing up in cosplay."

"What are you guys talking about?" Star asked as she stepped back into the truck.

"Ty and I have to run to Duck Key in the morning to pick up a couple cases of Key limes. It's a long drive, so don't worry about…"

Before I finished my sentence, Star interrupted. "Count me in. What time do we leave?

Color me surprised. I was shocked by her willingness

to join us, especially on her only day off. Star avoided extra work whenever possible. She was hiding something. I just knew it.

"It's an eight-hour round trip. You know that, right?"

"No problem at all. I'm always up for a road trip," she said with certainty. "Anything I can do to help with the business. That's my number one priority."

I knew she was lying at this point. "What's the real reason? Spill it."

"All right, all right," she said as she exhaled. "My Aunt Millie and Norma are stopping by tomorrow. Combine them with my mother, and our home becomes insufferable. You have to take me with you. I'm begging you, please."

For Star to give up her only day off, I knew she meant business. I could only imagine how annoyed her mom and aunts made her. They annoyed her enough to volunteer spending eight hours in the car with Ty and me.

"It's settled, then," I said as I smiled. "We should leave around 11 a.m. tomorrow morning. Everyone good with that?"

"Let's say 10 a.m., to be safe," Ty added.

"Safe for what?" Star asked as her ears perked up.

"I want to ensure we have enough time at Comic Fest before the crowds hit."

Star looked puzzled as she had no idea what she'd fully signed up for. "Wait, what?"

Strangely enough, I looked forward to driving to Duck Key with Star and Ty. Since my prodigal son-like return to Sunny Shores, I focused the majority of my time on work. Taking a road trip with two of my closest friends provided a much needed escape from the norm.

After stopping for coffee and snacks at Bert's convenience store, we began our trip south. The GPS estimated a 2:30 p.m. arrival at the Key Largo Trade and Convention Center. We planned to stop by Nerd Fest. ..I mean Comic Fest for a couple of hours, then head to Turtle Key.

"Be careful back there. Try not to get anything on my seats," Ty said as we headed southbound on Interstate 95. Ty recently bought a new car. His new Jeep was the first major purchase of his since passing the CPA exam. He was very particular and anal about it. "I'm not sure why you had to get a 44 ounce Big Gulp with red fruit punch."

Star shrugged as she sipped on her enormous drink.

As I turned around and smiled at Star, my mouth dropped when I noticed the outrageous amount of snacks she'd purchased from the gas station. It was enough to share between the three of us. She didn't seem the type to want to share, though.

"Geez Louise, Star. Do you think you bought enough snacks?"

"It's long car ride. Give me a break."

Before I could respond, my phone rang.

"Who's that?" Star asked.

"I'm not sure. The area code is 239."

Star pulled her phone out and worked her magic. "According to Google, area code 239 is Southwest Florida. Marathon and Key West area."

I answered the call, since it originated in the area we were visiting. It couldn't be a coincidence, right?

"OK. Thanks for the heads up. We'll see you then."

Smitty's supplier, Frank Stone, had called to inform me of a change in plans.

"Bad news," I said as I hung up the phone. "The guy we are getting the limes from—"

"Key limes, you mean."

"Yes, Star, Key limes. He needs to meet us earlier than planned because of a family emergency. That gives us very little time to stay at Comic Fest."

"Oh darn," Star blurted out. "Maybe next year, right, Ty?"

"We could do it after, on the way back," Ty said as he tried to compromise. "The convention is open until eight."

"That gives Kara less time to sleuth around."

"Sleuth around?" Ty said as he looked at me, confused. "Kara?"

Star laughed. "She didn't tell you the real reason we're on this wild-goose-chase of a trip."

I broke down and explained everything to Ty. Surprisingly enough, he understood and remained supportive. I thought of a compromise.

"We can drop Ty off at the convention and pick him

up on our way back," I explained as I turned to Ty. "This way you have more time at Comic Fest and feel less rushed."

"I guess that could work," Ty agreed. "Next time you have to come with me, OK?"

"You got it," I reassured him. "Promise."

After we picked up a couple of cases of Key limes from Frank, we headed north to Duck Key. I pulled out the former address of John Harmon from my purse and entered it into the GPS. Neither of us knew what to expect once we got there. The slight possibility of finding a clue fueled my desire, no matter how silly the idea.

"This is it," Star said as we pulled in front of the driveway. "778 San Juan Street."

The house we arrived at looked nothing like I'd pictured in my mind. The place stood much smaller than I imagined. The house was painted light pink with off-white trim and stood on stilts. The yard looked overgrown and unkempt. Apparently, the current owner lacked the funds for a lawn mower or landscaping services.

"What now?" Star asked as she parked the car by the mail box. "Looks like no one's home."

The place looked abandoned, and I wondered if anyone currently lived there. The house emitted a creepy vibe. My gut instinct warned me to turn away, but I ignored it as usual. Normally, listening to my gut resulted in gaining a few pounds.

"We've come too far to turn back now," I said as I bravely stepped out of the car. "Let's knock on the door and see if anyone's home."

"How about you knock on the door, and I stay here with the car running."

Star endured my obsession with solving the case and remained a good sport the entire time. So in an effort to avoid pressing my luck with her, I shook my head in agreement. As my grandma would say, "Choose your battles wisely." Besides if things went south, I might need a getaway driver.

I held my breath as I rang the door bell. As the tone echoed behind the door, I tapped my foot on the front porch. What questions would I ask? No clue. I failed to think that far ahead, so I figured I'd wing it.

I stood in front of the faded pink door a few minutes with no answer. I looked over at the window, and it appeared the lights were on inside. Either way, it seemed clear that no one was going to answer. So I walked down the front steps and headed back to the car.

Halfway between the house and the car, the door to the home slammed open, making a thundering sound.

"What in the blue hell do you want?" a voice screamed out from behind.

I turned around and saw a man standing in the door way looking directly at me. By the looks of his messy hair, he just woke from a nap or was drunk, maybe both. I noticed him stumbling out the door, dressed in a stained tank-top and ripped jean shorts. In one hand he held a cigarette, in the other, a red solo cup.

I shivered before I responded, mainly because I spotted a shotgun propped up against the door. I wanted more than anything to solve the case, but I wouldn't go so far as to risk my life. This man seemed crazier than a caged coon.

"Sorry to bother you, sir, but my friend and I were searching for information on a man who once lived here."

I turned in an effort to acknowledge Star and waved

at her. She responded by nodding her head and lifting her cell phone in the air. Star wished to inform the crazy looking man that 911 was only a phone call away.

"You better not be referring to that bastard, John Harmon."

I grinned in an attempt to lighten his mood. "Unfortunately, that's him."

"I've nothing to say about that crook."

"Well," I continued. "Someone murdered him last week in Sunny Shores."

"Good riddance," the man said as he chugged his drink. "That jerk had it coming."

Great, I thought as I listened to the man vent his frustrations about John Harmon. Yet another person who wanted John dead. The suspect list grew larger than the population of Florida.

"John Harmon knowingly sold me this lemon."

"This lemon?"

"I'm talking about this piece of crap house I bought from him. That man lied about the condition of this house. He failed to mention all the structural issues the house contained. He even went so far as to pay-off the home inspector."

The more he spoke, the larger the vein protruding from his head grew. As he shouted out his true feelings for John Harmon, he inched closer and closer to the shotgun. I couldn't tell if it was intentional or not, but I wasn't going to dilly-dally around and find out.

"How do you know that?" I asked as I continued to slowly walk backwards to the car.

"I confronted the home inspector at Tyson's bar one night. I bought him enough rounds of beer until he confessed the true story."

"Did you ever try to confront Mr. Harmon after you discovered the truth?"

"Why would I waste my time with him? There's nothing I could do. My debt from this home prevented me from getting a lawyer. I couldn't afford one if I tried. He ruined me financially," he explained as sweat dripped from his forehead. "After my wife and I purchased the house, the cost of repairs put a large stress on our marriage. We fought daily, and I gained thirty pounds in the process. My wife eventually divorced me. This whole mess started with that crook. He ruined my life."

At this point, the man was visibly upset. He looked like a ticking time-bomb set to explode at any time. I didn't plan to stick around for the impending explosion.

"I apologize for disturbing you. We'll be on our way now," I said as I turned away and marched towards the car.

"Stay the hell away from here and never mention his name again," he shouted as he went inside and slammed the door behind him.

I rushed back to the car without glancing back at him. We wore out our welcome, and we needed to press the eject button. My plan didn't involve getting shot in Duck Key.

Before I sat down in the car, a voice called out from the driveway next door. A short, elderly lady emerged from the bushes. The lady wore gardening gloves and held a pair of trimming shears in her hand.

"Another person with a potential weapon in reach," I thought. "What kind of neighborhood did we step into?"

"Pardon my intrusion, but I overheard your conver-sation with my neighbor," she said as she removed her gloves. She reached out and shook my hand. "I'm Nancy Thurman."

"Hi Nancy, I'm Kara Summers. It's nice to meet you. My friend Star is in the car over there."

She placed her gloves and trimming shears down on the ground. Then she reached into her pocket and pulled out a small piece of cloth. The woman took a deep breath and pressed the cloth against her forehead.

"It's hotter than the surface of the sun out here. Why don't you two come inside for a spell and cool off? How does a fresh glass of sweet tea sound?"

"Sound great," I said as I motioned to Star to get out and join us.

As we followed Nancy into her home, Star whispered, "Do you think she meant Long Island Ice Tea?

"I've lived in this house for almost twenty years. My ears perked up when you mentioned Mr. Harmon's name. I haven't heard that name in years. I'm sorry to hear of his passing."

"What do you remember about him?"

"To be honest, I rarely spoke with the man. His wife, on the other hand, was a sweet woman. She would talk my ear off for hours," she said as she took a sip from her glass of tea. "The Lord took that young lady too soon. Even now, the thought of her accident breaks my heart."

"I'm not sure if you heard or not, but John died last week. Someone burned him alive inside his food truck."

"Oh my," she said as she shook her head in disbelief. "I do recall you telling my neighbor of his murder, although I didn't realize how gruesome it was."

"It wasn't pretty, that's for sure," Star added.

"Can you recall anyone in town who hated John or had issues with him?"

"I honestly couldn't tell you, dear," she said as scratched her head. "I do remember fighting and screaming coming from their home, after his wife died?"

I perked up. "Fighting? Who with?"

"His son, I believe."

"Son?" Star and I both shouted in unison.

"Yes," Nancy said. "They had a son. I'm guessing he was around your age. He was a smart and handsome fellow. Although I'm not sure what happened to him. I recall him moving away before John left."

What had almost been a bust of a trip actually proved useful. In light of this discovery, I had to reconsider everything I thought I knew in regard to the case. The news of John Harmon having a biological son turned the case upside down, as well as inside out.

There was only one question that mattered.

"Who was John Harmon's son?"

"**M**y head," I said as I woke. I dozed off immediately once I got home. With everything going on, I hadn't had a good night's sleep in days. "What time is it?" I picked up my phone to check the time. "9:30 already?"

I couldn't believe I'd dozed off. I had so much to do around the house. What was crazier than that was that I had six missed calls on my phone. Four of them were from Will, alone. The other two calls were from Chief Martin and Ty.

"What could the chief want?"

My curiosity wouldn't allow me to go to bed without knowing the reason for Sam Martin calling. It had to have been important. In a small town like Sunny

Shores, calling someone after nine was considered rude. Manners aside, I needed to know.

"Hi Sam. It's me, Kara. I'm sorry I missed your call, but I fell asleep early tonight."

"Kara, I'm glad you called back. There's been a new discovery in the case."

"Oh, really?" I perked up quickly.

"You know how Tom's been missing? We found him tonight."

"That's a relief."

"Not exactly," he said as his voice changed to a more somber tone. "We found him, but he's dead."

My mood changed from hopeful to gloomy in a matter of seconds. Three deaths in less than one week. It was just too much.

"His body was found at the Motel 6 in Ocala. He was discovered by the maid early this morning. He suffered what appears to be a stab wound to the chest. The maid found him in a pool of his own blood. Not a pretty sight."

"Oh, my. Who do you think could have done it? Do you think it's connected to the Harmon case?"

"It's too early to tell. It does appear that he's been dead for over 48 hours. At this point, I wouldn't rule anything out," he said as he took a deep breath. "Nothing makes sense anymore." All of a sudden, my mind switched focus. I thought about Will. "Does Will know? Tom was his business partner. He's been worried sick about him."

"I'm not sure. Look, Kara, the reason I called was to warn you. If this is related to the Harmon case, it proves that the killer will stop at nothing to cover his tracks. This person means business, serious business. I don't want you caught in the crossfire."

"Sure, Sam. I understand."

"I'm being serious about this, Kara. I could lose my job giving this type of information to a civilian before the investigation is complete. This action alone goes against our code, but I know you too well. You've done some great detective work on this case, frankly. I'm rather impressed. It needs to stop before you get hurt. I need you to promise me you will back away from this case. Promise?"

"I promise." At this point, I was being truthful. Too many people had gotten hurt, and the killer was not one step closer to being captured. The responsible thing to do would be to walk away.

"Good," he said while sounding surprised I didn't resist. "Look, I've got to run. I'm going to send a squad car by to check up on you. In the meantime, be careful and call me if anything seems suspicious."

I easily hopped up from the couch and walked around the house. I checked each and every door and window, making sure every entry point was locked.

The phone rang again, immediately startling me to the point I jumped. I was anxious and on edge after hearing the news of Tom's death.

"Are you okay? I tried calling you earlier. It's not like you not to answer," Ty said. "You know how I worry."

"I know. I know," I said, still trying to catch my breath. "Listen, I've got big news."

"Hold that thought," he said, interrupting me before I could continue. "I've been searching the Internet all night using John's real name, and I found a big clue."

"You did? What is it?"

"I found a photo. Not only of him, but his son as well."

"You did? Who's his son? Can you recognize him?"

"No, not really. The photo is about ten years old."

"What's the photo of?"

"I found a listing on Craigslist where John was selling a boat of his. Attached to the listing was a photo of him with his son in front of the boat."

"Send it to me. I'll hang up while you do it. Call me back, okay?"

"Will do."

I felt like a kid on Christmas Eve. I stared at the phone, waiting impatiently for the text to arrive. I hoped the photo would be the clue we needed to finally identify the killer.

Knock, knock, knock. I felt startled once again, as someone was banging on the front door. Without a second thought, I reached over behind the couch and picked up my aluminum bat as I walked toward the door; with each step, I gripped the bat tighter and tighter.

I sighed in relief once I looked out the peephole. It was only Will.

"Hey. I wasn't expecting you this evening," I said as I opened the door to greet him.

"I apologize for coming unannounced, but I was getting worried about you. I tried calling you a few times, but you didn't answer. With all the craziness going around in town, I thought I'd check up on you. Hope you don't mind."

"No, not at all. I'm sorry I didn't answer, but it's been a crazy day. Everything going on with the case, Ty's news, the thing with Tom—"

Before I could finish, Will interjected. "Don't worry about Tom. I spoke with him this afternoon."

"Wait, what?" I knew I was sleep deprived, but what Will was saying didn't make sense.

"He's fine. Apparently, he was dealing with some family issues and has been in Atlanta for the last couple days. Although he's not sure of when he'll be able to come back," Will explained. "From the sound of it, it might be a while."

My intuition began to sound off sirens. What was he talking about? None of it made sense.

Before I could process it all, the text alert on my phone went off. I looked down at my phone and it was Ty. "Can you excuse me for just one minute? I need to run upstairs for a bit, but you can have a seat on the couch. I'll be right back."

"Okay…"

Will appeared confused and perplexed by the way I acted. He wore a puzzled look on his face as he slowly made his way to the couch. Tension thickened in the air.

Skipping every other step, I walked quickly up the stairs. I entered my room and closed the door behind me. I took a deep breath as I sat on the bed and opened Ty's message.

The photo loaded slowly, for what seemed like an eternity. Once fully downloaded, I examined it. The photo was precisely what Ty described. I focused on the boy in the photo. While he did look familiar, I failed to properly identify him. I kept staring, hell-bent on figuring it out.

Right before the point of giving up, I glanced momentarily at the boat. It was at that point I discovered I was focusing on the wrong detail. The real clue of the photo wasn't the boy. The real answer was the boat itself. But more importantly, the name.

The Salty Mutt

My heart sank quickly, like an anchor. All the puzzle pieces in my brain started to piece together. The killer's identity was now obvious. He was sitting in my living room.

"Is everything OK in there?" Will's voice called out from the other side of my bedroom door.

My heart began to race as I realized the possibility of a murderer being outside my door. Only a two inch slab of wood separated us. I didn't like my odds.

"I'm good," I said as I tried to cover up the nervousness in my voice. I was unsuccessful in that attempt as my voice shot up a few octaves. "I'll be down in a sec."

"This is crazy," I whispered to myself as I tried to convince myself I was wrong. The notion that Will murdered those innocent people seemed ridiculous. Every time Will and I hung out, he appeared normal. How could I not have noticed something strange about him?

"I have this crazy story to tell you about the loony dude that paints on the boardwalk. You'll love it, I'm sure," he said as he continued to stand outside my door. Could this guy not take a hint?

"Willie?" I asked.

"Yeah, that's him."

Immediately, my mind shifted gears. I recalled the

last thing Willie said during our conversation the other morning.

"Keep your friends close, but keep your enemies closer."

What I thought at the time was incoherent rambling was actual brilliant. Willie made perfect sense.

It suddenly occurred to me why Will wanted to spend so much time with me. He wanted to keep an eye on my investigation. That was how he kept one step ahead of me at all times. He only pretended to like me, so he could prevent me from getting too close to solving the murder.

At first, my heart sank at the notion that he'd used me. He fractured my already fractured ego. That feeling quickly dissipated as I remembered a killer stood outside my door.

24

I could sense Will's impatience growing, but I needed to be sure my assumption stood correct. But how?

An idea popped into my head. I walked over to my dresser and searched frantically. "It's here somewhere. I know it."

"Kara?" Will said as I heard him touch the door knob.

"Ah ha," I exclaimed as I reached out and retrieved the thing I was looking for. It was the slip of paper where Will wrote down his number. I carefully examined the W on it and compared it to the W on the suicide note. It was a match.

"Bingo," I shouted out. Although I felt proud I put the pieces together, the realization that a murderer stood in my house took me back to reality.

At that moment, Will opened the door and walked into my room. I smiled nervously. No doubt I looked as if I had something to hide.

"Umm...I'm not feeling too well," I said as I scooted back away from him. "If you don't mind, I'm going to bed. I'll call you in the morning."

Will continued to inch closer to me. I felt uncomfortable as he clearly missed the hint of me wanting him to leave.

"It's you, isn't it," I asked as I glanced out the corner of my eye. I tried to locate my cell phone. I hoped I could pick it up, nonchalantly, of course. "Will Green."

"Will Green, who's that?" he said. His tone sounded nervous, as if he was trying to hide something.

I was fed up and didn't care anymore. I'd grown sick of people, especially men, lying to me.

"Stop lying to me, Will. I know you did it."

"Did what, Kara? What are you getting at?"

"Don't play stupid with me. You murdered them. John Harmon, Missy, and even Todd. It all makes sense now."

"I think you need to have a seat on the bed. You've obviously gone mad," he said as he continued to inch closer to me. "You need to calm down."

"The extra propane tank wasn't ordered by Todd. It was ordered by you. You knew because your father was an avid smoker, he'd light the truck up with one puff. That's why you sent him a text to meet you at the Mama Mia Food truck. It's also why you slashed Chris's tires, so he would be late. Leaving you and John alone."

"That's crazy."

"You figured it would be ruled an accident. Grove Park provided the perfect venue. No security cameras. But because I had video, it ruined it all. So you had to throw everyone off your scent by killing Missy and staging it as a suicide. Too bad the hand-writing matches yours and not hers."

He continued to move closer to me. I looked down and noticed his mud-stained tennis shoes. My mind flashed back to the night my window was broken. I didn't put it together at the time, but Will's shoes were muddy. The person that broke my window stomped through my flower bed, which was wet from an afternoon shower.

"You broke my window that night. Your shoes were muddy from walking through my garden. If you were truly just jogging on the street, why where your shoes muddy?"

"What do you want from me, Kara? What do you want me to say?"

"I want you to admit you killed those people. Admit you're truly a monster."

I reached over and picked up my phone and starting swiping my finger across it. Will responded by slapping it out my hand. He laughed as it slid across my bedroom floor.

"OK, you win," he said as he looked directly into my eyes. "I killed them. You have no idea the kind of man my father was. He didn't deserve a happy ending. Not after he took my mother away from me."

"I thought that your mother was killed in a car accident. The police report stated that the accident was the fault of the other driver."

"It was entirely my father's fault. My dad had been drinking all day and was drunk. I remember to this day how bad he was that night. My mother begged and pleaded for him to stay home, but he kept insisting he was fine. She only rode with him because she was worried about him."

"There was nothing in the police report that would point to a DUI."

"Of course it was covered up. My father was running for state senate at the time."

"How could you murder your own father?"

"My father was the true monster, don't you ever forget that. All I did was exterminate the monster and make things right again. I never planned on killing Todd and Missy. Those two were in the wrong place at the wrong time. Kind of like you."

"I don't understand. Why do this now? After all these years, why come to Sunny Shores? Why bring the pain back into your life?"

"I was doing fine on my own. I started a new life in Jacksonville and was happy. It wasn't until the letter came that all those years of bottled up frustration came pouring back out."

"What letter?"

Will reached into the back pocket of his jeans and pulled out a worn, folded up letter. He unfolded it slowly and handed it to me. "This letter."

I opened the envelope and took out the letter. Folded up inside the letter was a family photo, of John, Missy, and Chris. The three of them appeared to be very happy.

"When I saw the photo and read the letter, I grew angry thinking about how happy my father was with his new life. He had disposed of my mother and me, acted like we didn't exist."

As he continued to talk, I looked around the room and tried to find a way out. It was no use, as he'd cornered me. I didn't want to die, not that night, especially with my hair looking like this.

"I wish you would have stayed out of this and minded your own business," he said as he pulled a gun from his back pocket. "I didn't want to have to do this."

I closed my eyes as I feared the worst. Maybe he was right. Maybe I should have minded my own business.

I heard a loud thud, but it wasn't a gun shot. I opened my eyes to see what happened.

To my surprise, my friend Ty stood over the unconscious body of Will. Ty looked heroic as he held my baseball bat in his hand.

He smiled. "What do you think of my swing now?"

I walked over and put my arms around him. A flurry of emotions rushed through me as I held him tight. I whispered into his ear, "Thank you."

"I started to worry when you didn't answer my call. So to keep my mind at ease, I drove by your house. When I saw your door wide open, I knew something was wrong."

"How's that?"

"You're always screaming at Star and me to keep the door shut on the truck."

A few minutes later, Sam Martin and two other officers arrived at the scene. Ty and I gave our stories to Sam, while the other two police officers cuffed Will. As they stood him up, he regained consciousness.

"What proof do you have? None of what you told me earlier would hold up in court," he said as he struggled with the officers.

"That might be true," I said as I walked over and picked up my cell phone off the floor. "I have something better."

"What's that?" Will asked.

I smiled. "Your confession."

When I picked my phone up previously, Will assumed I attempted to make a call. Unfortunately for him, my plans were different. I knew I wouldn't have time to call anyone, so I opened up the voice recorder app on my phone and hit the record button.

Our entire conversation, which included his confession, was recorded.

"Good work," Sam said as he winked and smiled. "Maybe we will make a detective out of you yet."

As they took Will away, I handed Sam the letter Will received in the mail. It was the same letter that started this whole mess in the beginning. Who knew? It may prove useful in the future, because one question still remained.

Who sent the letter to Will?

25

The next morning at work, there was a noticeably lighter mood around Grove Park. A dark cloud of fear and anxiety no longer hovered over the park. I could tell the other food truck owners felt a sense of relief. The one person that threatened our safety was behind bars. Things could finally get back to normal. Well… as normal as possible in our quirky town.

For me personally, I felt better than I had in months. Ever since my father died, I felt emptiness inside. It was a void that nothing at the time could fill, not even my ex or career aspirations.

There was a chance the void left by my father would never be filled, but for the first time in a while I felt happy.

By helping solve the murder of John Harmon, I felt a sense of personal accomplishment. But even more than that, I felt like I was helping my father's legacy live on.

Getting all the prep work in that morning was almost impossible. Every few minutes, another person would stop by and congratulate me on solving the case. Of course, I'd correct them by telling them I couldn't have done it without help from my friends. I felt they deserved just as much credit.

"How in the world are we ever going to get anything done," Star said as she threw her hands up in frustration. "We open in less than an hour. Why aren't you stressing out?"

I'll admit that seeing Star run around the truck like a chicken with its head cut off tickled my funny bone. It was encouraging to see Star so invested. When I first met her, she didn't seem to care about anything. That role was reserved for me normally, but I felt a sense of calm come over me. I'd almost forgotten how that felt.

"It's okay, Star," I said as I smiled. "I called Ty and asked if he would come in and help out today. He'll be here soon."

"Oh great. Another visitor," Star said as Carlos and his wife Maria approached the truck. "Keep it quick, Kara."

Carlos and his wife walked up, holding hands. They both appeared in a great mood, and Carlos wore a big smile.

"Carlos and I wanted to stop by and say thank you," Maria said. "Carlos hasn't stopped talking about how proud he was of you and your friends."

"Guilty," Carlos said, shaking his head in agreement. "Only guilty of that, just to be clear."

We all laughed.

"Now that the spot at the beach entrance is open again, you should take it back. I'm positive the other food truck owners would agree. We could take a vote," I said. Carlos deserved it.

"It's funny you should say that," Carlos replied with a mischievous look on his face. "It's already been decided."

"Really? That's great."

"I made a few calls to members of the city council. With the help of a certain city council member, it was decided that the spot was mine. The only catch was that the other food truck owners agree."

So that was why Carlos was so happy. He was finally going to regain the spot that was rightfully his. The outcome was great news.

"Congratulations, Carlos."

"Tell her what you told them," Maria said.

"I told them no. I didn't want it," Carlos said.

At first, I thought he was kidding. The only thing Carlos talked about for weeks was losing the spot. Why would he tell them no?

"Why? I don't understand," I said, confused.

"I told them that you deserved it. If the spot was mine, I wanted to give it to you," Carlos said as he handed me a sheet of paper.

I scanned over the sheet curiously. The document was full of signatures, but I couldn't tell the purpose.

"What's this?"

"This is a petition to grant you the spot. It's been signed by every other food truck owner in the park."

Maria interrupted, "Except for the Cover Your Buns

hot dog truck, of course. The owner was a bit tied up for the moment."

"I don't know what to say," I said. "Thank you."

"I know what to say," Star said. "It's time to hire more help."

"I lost three years of my life to a crime I didn't commit. Because of you, that didn't happen again. You helped clear my name, and always gave me the benefit of the doubt during the process. It's the least I can do," Carlos said.

I don't find myself speechless very often, but the words escaped me, and I didn't know what to say.

"It's very sweet of you, but I thought you depended on the extra business that spot brought. You have a family to feed, and I don't want to take away from that."

"We'll be fine," Maria said. "Carlos is getting too old to be working so hard. That's a young person's game now. Besides, the added stress was killing him. I'd rather have him around for a long time. That's more important to me than money."

Carlos put his arm around Maria, giving her a kiss on the cheek. When his lips pressed against her face, you could see the love she had for him glow through her smile. No amount of money could top that.

"Besides, I've penny pinched and saved over the last few years. The reduced workload and schedule will be nice," he said. "Plus, now you can save more money. We really want to see you open your own shop someday. I believe in my heart that cooking's what you were meant to do," Carlos said.

"And don't forget solving crimes too. She's not so bad at that," Star said.

"She certainly has a knack for that," Carlos said. "You should be able to move to the new spot sometimes next week. The city still has to clean up a few things first. But after that, it's all yours."

As soon as Carlos left, I tried to finish the last of my preparations. Before I could begin, I spotted Sam Martin marching toward my truck.

"What now?" I thought as he approached. He had a look on his face that reminded me of one my parents gave me. It was a look of anger sprinkled with a dash of disappointment. I saw that look many times growing up.

"Kara, what you did was incredibly dumb," Sam said, scolding me like a parent would a misbehaved child. "Not only, that but it was idiotic and dangerous. What if he hurt you? Or even worse…"

"With all due respect, I did what needed to be done. John Harmon was a terrible man, but he didn't deserve the death sentence his son dished out."

"I'm not disagreeing with that. What you're saying is justified."

"So what's the issue? Why am I on trial here for wanting to do the right thing?"

"The issue is I don't want to see you get hurt, Kara. You're like a daughter to me. I've already lost your dad. I don't want anything happening to you. I couldn't live with myself."

"I never meant to upset you, but the police department ignored the evidence and turned the other way." The frustration of the police department turning a blind-eye to the investigation bugged me. "I don't understand why more wasn't done."

"The mayor cut the department's resources and budget last month. He's pressured me to think of the economic health of the town over an individual. It wasn't right."

"I understand." With Sam being newly appointed as Chief of Police by the mayor, I couldn't imaging the pressure involved. Mayor Roy held power over Sam. Sam followed orders, like any good subordinate would.

"With that being said, I'm very proud of you. What you did was brave and showed guts. Your father would have been proud. I'm sure of that."

"Thank you, Sam. That means a lot."

I felt the tears building up behind my eye lids, while I was trying to keep it together emotionally. "No more meddling from me. I'll keep my nose out of police business from now on."

Sam laughed. "We both know that isn't true."

"Why do you say that?"

"You're your father's daughter, and there's no denying that. You have so much of your father in you it's insane."

"If you decide to play Nancy Drew again, just promise me one thing."

"Sure. Anything you ask."

"Be careful," he said as he placed his hand on my

shoulder. "Keep me in the loop. OK? Your father and I worked well together. I'm sure the same could be said for us."

"I promise."

From behind Sam's back, he pulled a thick vanilla folder out and placed it on the counter in front of me. He took a deep breath, pushing it towards me.

"The mayor, in his infinite wisdom, ordered all unsolved case files closed. No exceptions. The department is under strict orders to cease any and all investigations on these cases. My hands are tied."

"Is that what I think it is?"

"This is everything we have on your father's murder. The folder contains all testimonies, evidence, witness reports, and notes regarding his case. Most of it compiled by myself."

I couldn't take my eyes off the case file. The folder was stuffed to the brim with papers and needed a large rubber band to keep it closed. It was obvious by its size that a lot of time and effort went into investigating it.

"I spent too much time and energy trying to solve this case for the mayor to try shutting it down. I want answers as much as you, but my hands are tied." He leaned over closer to me and whispered, "But yours aren't."

I stood there motionless. My mind was crammed with hundreds of unanswered questions, mostly surrounding the circumstances of my father's death. Now, right in front of me, was a case file, full of answers. Little did I know, the file would lead to even more questions.

"Can't you get in trouble for this?"

"The mayor would have a hard time firing his Chief of Police for making a small mistake. I'm human, after all. If I happened to forget a case file on a counter while getting coffee, that's a simple mistake, right?"

I smiled. "No one's perfect. Mistakes happen."

"I have to run," he said as he backed away from the food truck. "Happy sleuthing."

26

A sense of relief and calmness flowed through my body. Nobody could ruin the near-perfect day. My bubble popped when the mayor waddled himself over to my window.

"Seems you've been quite busy, sweetheart," Mayor Roy said as he leaned his arm against my counter.

Roy reached into his shirt pocket, pulling out a hand-kerchief. While winking at Star, he took the handker-chief and wiped the sweat from his forehead. To say the man was disgusting would have been putting it lightly. I imagined by just existing, he'd work up a sweat.

Star, in her effort to ignore him, turned her back and continued working. A smart move, for sure.

"Mr. Colt… I mean Roy, what can I do for you?" I asked, correcting myself in the nick of time.

"That was mighty fine detective work. It's a shame you're wasting all that talent on this silly dream of yours," he said.

I wanted to smack the smug look off his face, but I resisted. Barely.

"Don't you think it's time you stop this foolishness and regain some sense? I called in some favors to the university. Pulled some strings, if you will. You can re-enroll in August, and only be one semester behind."

"I appreciate what you're trying to do, but I—"

"Don't you worry your pretty little head off about Dusty. He forgives you and is willing to work past this silliness of the last few months."

Roy turned around and faced two men who were waiting in line behind him. "Women, right?" The two men shrugged and tried to remain neutral by staying out of it.

"First of all, Dustin and I are never getting back

together. I broke up with him for a reason."

"I was just trying to—"

"And furthermore, my business is not a silly little dream to me. I've worked hard to build this business, and it's doing well. Who cares if I don't go to law school and become a lawyer?"

"Like the world needs more lawyers," Star said, interjecting her thoughts from the back of the truck.

"Settle down, sweetheart."

I'd had enough of his sexist and antiquated attitude at that point. "Roy, if you're not going to order, I'm going to have to ask you to step aside. I have other customers to serve."

"These things have a way of working themselves out in the end," he said as he grinned. "You can work this out with Dusty in person. He's coming back to town in a few weeks."

As he walked off, he made sure to mumble one last insult our way. "Must be their time of the month."

Before I could process the news of Dustin returning to town, Star rushed over and pushed me playfully. "Who was that?"

"You know the mayor. Don't be silly."

"I'm not talking about the mayor," she said. "I'm referring to the stranger standing in front of me. The Kara I knew would've never done that."

"People change," I replied. "Maybe it's the new me?"

"I like it." Star smiled as she walked over to greet the next customer in line.

"I'm not going to lie," I said with a huge smile on my face. "It felt good."

The old Kara would've let Roy run over her. He would have put her in a foul mood and ruined the rest of her day. Not today. Not anymore.

The back door to the truck opened and Star emerged from the outside, with Ty in tow behind her.

"Look who finally decided to show up," she said as she placed her apron on.

"I got here as quick as I could," Ty explained. "It's been a crazy morning."

"He's been too busy signing autographs and kissing babies," Star said.

Ty showed up late because everyone he encountered

stopped him to discuss the incident from the night before. His heroic actions were not something common in our little town. Since news traveled fast, it wasn't long before everyone in town knew of how awesome he was.

"The town hero, eh?" I said, teasing him.

Ty, modest by nature, tried to change the subject. He was never one to gloat or brag. The flushed look on his face displayed how nervous the attention made him.

"Be back in a second," he said. Ty picked up a trash bag that was less than half-full. "I need to take out the trash."

As Ty walked outside, I watched him through the window. It wasn't a few seconds after he put the bag in the dumpster when another town member stopped to talk to him. I couldn't take my eyes off him as I watched him recall the story. The gestures he made while telling his story were cute. I grinned feverishly.

Star glanced over my way, immediately noticing my enamored gaze out the window. When she noticed who I was looking at, she said, "That dork's not so bad, is he?"

"No. No, he's not." I shook my head in agreement, but broke my gaze.

"He went from being a nerd to a bad-ass. He's kind of sexy now."

"He sure is," I said. "There's something different about him now, although I can't put my finger on what it is."

Star laughed. "I told you so."

I played dumb. "Told me what?'

"That you two were more than friends."

"Whatever," I replied, trying to play it off and seem cool. "Go make today's specialty drink. No more playing cupid for the day.

"Yes ma'am. Cherry limeade as usual." Star shrugged her shoulders and walked to the back of the truck.

I couldn't stop thinking about Ty and how he saved my life. Maybe Star was right. There may have been more to my feelings for Ty than I realized. But who knows. There was still a lot of summer left. No need to rush anything.

What started out as a rough patch in my life ended up not being so bad after all. There was no denying that I hadn't accomplished the goals I'd originally set out for my life. Was it that big of a deal? Sure, I wasn't married, and I didn't have children, a six-figure job, or a fancy home. Everything I did have was not so bad. In fact, things were looking up for me.

I turned the negatives in my life around, turning them to positives. I had friends and family that were there for me, a growing business of my own, and I lived in a wonderful town. Life wasn't so bad.

"We're out of limes. What do you want me to do?" Star shouted. "All we have is a box full of lemons."

I smiled and immediately thought of Grandma's favorite quote: "When life gives you lemons…"

"Lemonade it is, then."

THANKS FOR READING

A message from Cassie...

I want to personally thank each and everyone of
you who took the time to read my book. I
encourage you to send any feedback you might
have to me. I also appreciate any reviews left on
Amazon. Also, be sure to check out my website. I
will often post chapter previews and other goodies.

I have also included a sneak peek of book 2,
Coconut Cream Confession at the back of this book.
It's up for pre-order on Amazon.

Contact me by email at cassie@cassierivers.com
Visit my website at www.cassierivers.com

Join my mailing list and receive a free mystery book. http://eepurl.com/cvJw5P

PREVIEW OF COCONUT CREAM CONFESSION

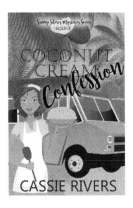

Available for Pre-Order Click Here to View on Amazon

COCONUT CREAM CONFESSION

"What's that?" I asked as a loud scratching sound came from the back door.

Star's eyes lit up. "It must be Mr. Whiskers."

Star unofficially adopted a stray tabby cat, Mr. Whiskers, who hung out around Grove Park. The orange and white fur-ball visited our truck almost daily. Star left a bowl of water and a bowl of food at the back of the truck. Star wanted to take her home. However, her mother refused to allow her to have a cat due to her allergies.

Star's overall demeanor changed each time she encountered Mr. Whiskers. Most of the time, Star displayed a no nonsense, sassy attitude. That all changed when that cat came around. A loving and nurturing side of her emerged from the shadows each time Mr. Whiskers showed his furry face.

"That's sounds odd," Star said as we both looked at each other confused.

Mr. Whiskers often scratched gently on the door to alert Star he wanted attention or additional food. Something seemed different this time. He continued to scratch louder and louder. Instead of a soothing purr, a loud screech sounded out from behind the door.

Star walked over to the door and gave me a concerned look before opening it. As the door swung open, Mr. Whiskers shot into the truck like a bolt of lightning. He ran past Star and jumped onto the counter, while knocking two mixing bowls onto the floor.

"Get him out of here," I yelled as I watched cupcake batter pour onto the floor. "He's making a mess."

"I'll grab him," Star replied as she tried to cat the crazed cat. "Hold still, Mr. Whiskers!"

"What's with him today?"

Suddenly, my question was answered as the sound of

barking filled the air. Before Star could close the door, a dog jumped into the truck.

The dog was none other than Mrs. Trudy Watson's prized cocker spaniel, Pookie. His sudden appearance caused even more pandemonium as the two animals ran circles around the inside of the truck.

My jaw dropped as I watched all my prep work from that morning become a scattered mess on the floor. We both tried to stop them, but our efforts remained useless. The two animals went at it like caged UFC fighters.

"Pookie, get out here this instant," a woman's voice shouted out from outside the door.

I peeked out the corner of my eye to the back door. Trudy Watson stood outside, holding a leash in one hand and a cigarette in the other. She appeared as if she recently rolled out of bed as her hair was in rollers and wearing her fluffy bright pink robe.

The sound of Trudy's harsh tone and nasally voice caused Pookie to stop dead in her tracks. Pookie looked over at Trudy and then back at Mr. Whiskers. Pookie acted hesitant at first, but the dog decided to listen to her master as she walked over to the door.

The sudden distraction allowed Star to grab the cat and restrain him in her arms.

"What are you doing messing with that mangy cat," Trudy said as she attached the lease to Pookie's pink collar. "There's no telling what kind of disease you could get from it. I have a good mind to call animal control. Teach that pest a lesson."

"Excuse me," Star said as she became defense. "Maybe you should learn to keep your mutt on a leash? She's the one who caused all of this."

"Mutt? I'll have you know that Pookie is a prized and fully pedigreed English Cocker Spaniel from the Walsh Breed out of Oxford. She's hardly a mutt."

"If she's so dang important, why are you letting her run loose through Grove Park?"

"It wasn't my fault. My good-for-nothing freeloader of a brother let her loose," she said as she took a puff from her cigarette. "I let him sleep on my couch for free, and all I ask of him is to do one thing. His only job is to walk Pookie for me, and he can't even do that right. All he cares about is sleeping and bow hunting."

As the two of them continued to argue semantics, I stood there with my mouth wide open. I could only think of one thing. The massive mess. The only thought bouncing around my head was who would clean up the tremendous mess in my truck.

I wanted to cry as I thought about how much work was wasted that morning. Instead, I knew my duty was to try and diffuse the situation and act like an adult. I didn't need my only full-time employee arrested for assault.

"Ms. Watson, we apologize for the inconvenience. Come by another day, and your meal is on us."

I thought it a fitting compromise, since currently all the meals I'd prepared that morning were on the floor. Star looked as if she wanted to scream at me.

"Knock. Knock," another voice called out from behind Trudy.

I looked curiously as a red hat appeared in the doorway. Unfortunately for me, I realized Margaret Pettyjohn was the person under the red hat. It was a mix of impeccable timing and bad luck. Ms. Pettyjohn not only served as a town councilmember, but held the office of city health inspector as well.

"Hello, Ms. Pettyjohn," I said as I started to panic internally. "I hate to ask, but could you come back later. You've caught us at a bad time."

That was an understatement, to say the least. She not only caught us at a bad time, but caught us with our pants down as well. The inside of the Murder She Wrote food truck looked like the aftermath of a food fight.

Ms. Pettyjohn turned to face Trudy and said," I thought I smelled a foul stench in the air, but I didn't notice the fisherman cleaning their catch. But then you're here now. It all makes sense."

"You're lucky I didn't press charges, when I heard you and your friend were snooping around my property the other day."

"If your deadbeat brother wasn't two months behind on alimony payments and answered his phone, I wouldn't have to drop by unannounced."

Trudy turned her nose up and pretended to ignore Margaret's less than stellar greeting. "Let's go, Pookie. I didn't realize it was trash day already."

Ms. Pettyjohn shook her head in disgust as Trudy walked away. Ms. Pettyjohn mood turned to one of anger and she turned to me and said, "I didn't know you two were close. Makes sense, I guess."

Before I could respond, she stepped one foot inside my truck and looked around. She let out a loud sigh as she took out a notebook and began to scribble down notes. My heart skipped a beat each time she pushed her pencil against the paper.

"Is this the way you run your business?" She asked as she continued to scan the room with her eye brows raised. "I can't say I'm surprised, though."

"You're kidding, right?" Star responded as she continued to hold and comfort Mr. Whiskers. "Kara is an obsessive-compulsive person about cleaning. This is obviously an accident."

"Wait just a minute," Ms. Pettyjohn said as she adjusted her glasses. "You have a cat inside your food truck. You know that's a serious health code violation."

"This is all a big misunderstanding," I said as I motioned for Star to get the cat out of the truck. "I would never allow a pet inside my truck on normal conditions, but…"

"I'm standing here looking at it right now," she said as she began to write something down. "I've seen enough."

She tore off a sheet from her notepad and handed it to me. I glanced at it and discovered the note was a citation. I stood there in shock as I attempted to make sense of it.

"As of right now, I'm shutting you down. By order of section 110 – ordinance 2, you are hereby required to cease all business operations until a full inspection can be completed."

"Wait…what?"

"If you are caught conducting any business on these premises, you may permanently lose your business license.

"How long will that be?" I asked. "Can you come back by tomorrow?"

"Let me check my schedule," she said as she flipped through a few pages of her notebook. There was little doubt in my mind she was looking. "My next available slot is Friday, July 10th."

"That's almost two weeks away. Are you sure you can't come sooner? This is all one big mistake, I assure you."

"Not inspecting your business sooner was the big mistake," she said as she began to walk out the door. "Besides, it will probably take you two weeks to clean this disaster up. Look at the bright side. In a way, I'm doing you a favor."

As she walked away, Star and I stood in disbelief. With my business shut down during the two busiest weeks in the summer, what were we going to do?

I hope you enjoyed the preview. The book is available now for pre-order on Amazon.

CLICK HERE

Made in the USA
Middletown, DE
09 December 2018